D0916821

LAWRENCEBURG PUBLIC LIBRARY

FIGHTING FOR EQUALITY

INDIANA HISTORICAL SOCIETY PRESS
INDIANAPOLIS 2007

FIGHTING FOR EQUALITY

A Life of May Wright Sewall

RAY E. BOOMHOWER

I
B
SEWALL

© 2007 Indiana Historical Society Press

Printed in Canada

This book is a publication of the
Indiana Historical Society Press
450 West Ohio Street
Indianapolis, Indiana 46202-3269 USA
www.indianahistory.org
Telephone orders 1-800-447-1830
Fax orders 1-317-234-0562
Online orders @ shop.indianahistory.org

Portions of this book were previously published as *"But I Do Clamor": May Wright Sewall,
A Life, 1844–1920* (Indianapolis: Guild Press of Indiana, 2001).

The paper in this publication meets the minimum requirements of American National
Standard for Information Sciences—Permanence of Paper for Printed Library materials,
ASNI Z39. 48–1984

Library of Congress Cataloging-in-Publication Data

Boomhower, Ray E., 1959–
    Fighting for equality : a life of May Wright Sewall / Ray E. Boomhower.
        p. cm.
    ISBN-13: 978-0-87195-253-0 (cloth : alk. paper)
        1. Sewall, May Wright, 1844-1920. 2. Feminists—United States—Biography.
    3. Women social reformers—United States—Biography. I. Title.

HQ1413.S37B664 2007
305.420973—dc22

2007008517

No part of this publication may be reproduced, stored in or introduced into a retrieval system,
or transmitted, in any form or by any means (electronic, photocopying, recording, or otherwise),
without the prior written permission of the copyright owner.

12/11

Once again, for Megan.

"My country is the world, my countrymen are all mankind."

— *May Wright Sewall*

Fighting for Equality: A Life of May Wright Sewall is made possible through the generous support of the Lacy Foundation/LDI, Ltd.

Contents

Educator, reformer, women's rights pioneer May Wright Sewall.

HULTON ARCHIVE/GETTY IMAGES

Chapter 1

The Reformer

While preparing for classes one day on the third floor of a high school in Indianapolis, Indiana, a teacher received a visit from a well-known person: Zerelda Wallace, widow of former governor David Wallace and president of the Indiana chapter of the Woman's Christian Temperance Union, a group determined to help families torn apart by alcohol.

Wallace had come to the school to ask the teacher, May Wright Sewall, to sign a petition in favor of temperance that Wallace planned on presenting to the Indiana state legislature. Sewall was about to write her name on the document when she read that those who signed did not intend to "clamor" for any additional civil or political rights, including suffrage (the right to vote). "But I do clamor," Sewall said. She threw the petition on the floor and walked out of the room.

Although she refused to sign the temperance petition, Sewall later joined forces with Wallace to help found the Indianapolis Equal Suffrage Society, a group that sought equality for women during a time in American history when they were not allowed to vote and often could not own property. The society came about in large part due to the "open contempt" showed to Wallace by Hoosier legislators when she attempted to present her temperance petition. One lawmaker even went so far as to tell Wallace that since women had no political power, her document "might as well have been signed by 10,000 mice."

To make sure that those in power would pay attention, Sewall worked throughout her life on behalf of rights for women in the United

States—and around the world—during the late nineteenth and early twentieth centuries. She served as a valuable assistant to such nationally known suffragists (women who fought for the right to vote and other civil rights) as Susan B. Anthony and Elizabeth Cady Stanton. Sewall also gave the woman's movement a worldwide reach by working to create the International Council of Women, which brought together different women's clubs and organizations to work to improve life for their sex.

By the early 1900s, according to the influential *Harper's Bazaar* magazine, Sewall had attracted to her cause approximately five million women in eleven countries. She had become so famous that even royalty was impressed. During a garden party hosted by Great Britain's Queen Victoria during an International Council of Women meeting in London, a newspaper reported that although there were a number of women of royal birth at the occasion, Sewall was "the only one who made the court bow as if she were used to it."

Sewall's involvement in suffrage was but one part of her life. Viewed as a natural leader by others who spoke out for rights for women, she had been raised in Wisconsin by a family that encouraged her to better herself through education. Described as having a "powerful, dominant and queenly personality," Sewall became a leading citizen in Indianapolis after her move to the city to take a high school teaching job in 1874. She quickly won the loyalty of her Indianapolis students. A local newspaper even claimed that she was "more talked of in the homes of the city by the young persons who met her in class work than all the other members of the faculty."

Known as "a large woman of sturdy carriage," Sewall played a significant role in the history of Indianapolis. At first with her husband, the Harvard-educated Theodore Lovett Sewall, and later alone, she operated the influential Girls' Classical School. The private school provided hundreds of young women with the advanced education they

FROM THE COLLECTIONS OF THE LEW WALLACE STUDY AND MUSEUM, CRAWFORDSVILLE, INDIANA

In addition to being a leader in the Woman's
Christian Temperance Union's fight against
alcohol, Zerelda Wallace served as First Lady
of Indiana when her husband, David Wallace,
served as governor of the state beginning in 1837.

INDIANA HISTORICAL SOCIETY, P408

LIBRARY OF CONGRESS

In the late nineteenth and early twentieth centuries, women across the United States campaigned for the right to vote on the local level, including (top) this horse-drawn wagon full of suffragists in Hebron, Indiana, and (bottom) nationally in a parade down Pennsylvania Avenue in the nation's capital in Washington, D.C.

needed to go on to earn college degrees.

In her work at the school, Sewall championed reform not only for what women were taught, but for what they wore, establishing a "simple school dress" that allowed her students to participate in physical fitness exercises. One of her students, Charlotte Cathcart, noted that she and others may have forgotten what they learned in the classroom, but they never forgot Sewall.

The house where Sewall lived with her husband served as a place where people could come every week to discuss important issues of the day and hear talks by nationally known literary and political figures. *Harper's Bazaar* called the Sewalls' home "the social and literary centre of all Indiana." She also improved the city through her efforts to form such organizations as the Indianapolis Woman's Club, the Art Association of Indianapolis, and the Indianapolis Propylaeum. "Everybody who came near her was interesting to her," noted Mary Judah, a family friend.

Famed Indiana author Booth Tarkington boldly claimed that along with former president Benjamin Harrison and legendary poet James Whitcomb Riley, Sewall would have been chosen as one of Indianapolis's three most important citizens.

Sewall's efforts to improve life reached throughout the world. In addition to lecturing widely across the United States on behalf of women's rights, she also attempted to win people's support for another cause—world peace, an effort she called her "absorbing ideal." Following the motto "My country is the world, my countrymen are all mankind," Sewall promoted the cause of peace through membership in the American Peace Society and through her work with both the National Council of Women and the International Council of Women.

When World War I broke out in Europe in 1914 and many who had worked against war believed that their efforts had failed, Sewall refused to quit. To help promote the cause of peace, she called upon textbook publishers to eliminate patriotic language and to replace it with calls for brotherhood. Sewall also asked mothers to remove from their children's playrooms toys that might promote warfare.

Sewall's work for the peace movement continued in November 1915 when millionaire automobile manufacturer Henry Ford asked her to join him and others interested in ending the bloody war then raging in Europe between the Allies (England, France, and Italy) and the Central Powers (Germany and Austria-Hungary). Sewall became one of sixty people to join Ford aboard the *Oscar II*, a passenger ship that sailed for Norway in hopes of getting the soldiers out of the trenches and back home to their loved ones before Christmas.

The Ford expedition failed in its mission, and World War I dragged on until America entered the war in 1918 on the Allied side. But Sewall's other numerous local, national, and international achievements won for her a well-deserved reputation for having "the 'organizing touch.'"

A reporter noted that Sewall had a unique ability to get people to work together for a common cause. The reporter described her as "a sort of social clockmaker who gets human machinery into shape, winds it up and sets it to running."

Those who worked with her to win women the right to vote saw Sewall as a no-nonsense woman. Unknown to all but a few of her friends, however, Sewall led a secret life—one involving attempts to communicate with loved ones after their deaths. After her husband died from tuberculosis in 1895, Sewall at first attempted to forget her grief through hard work. Her journey into the spirit world began when she attended a meeting at Lily Dale, New York, two years after her husband passed away.

Although she had been determined to leave the area immediately after speaking at the meeting, a series of unexplained delays caused her to eventually meet with a medium, a person who claimed she could receive messages from the dead. Provided with a blank slate that never left her

As in political campaigns, supporters of a woman's right to vote used slogans, badges, and buttons like this one to promote their message.

INDIANA HISTORICAL SOCIETY, R368

hands, Sewall gave the medium a list of questions to be answered. Taking the slate back to her hotel room, Sewall was shocked to find that answers had mysteriously appeared on the slate. This experience, she said, gave her "actual knowledge, if not of immortality, at least of a survival of death."

Until her own death in 1920, Sewall claimed to be in almost constant contact with her deceased husband, who told her to be very cautious telling other people as they would not believe her. The few people to whom she related her adventures with the spiritual world all believed Sewall was mistaken in her belief that she could speak with the dead. Despite the negative reaction she received, Sewall wrote about her amazing experiences with spiritualism in a book titled *Neither Dead nor Sleeping*.

Sewall's good friend and fellow women's rights pioneer Grace Julian Clarke offered the best tribute to Sewall and what she represented to women everywhere when she said: "I never left Mrs. Sewall's presence without resolving to be more outspoken in good causes, more constant in their service, without a fresh resolve to let trivial concerns go and emphasize only really vital interests."

8

LIBRARY OF CONGRESS

NORTH WIND PICTURE ARCHVIES

*A Quaker minister and founder of the first female antislavery society,
Lucretia Mott (right) played a leading early role in the fight for women's rights
in the United States, including being a mentor to Elizabeth Cady Stanton (left),
who noted that Mott opened to her "a new world of thought."*

Chapter 2

The Teacher

On July 11, 1848, in the *Seneca County Courier* newspaper, a notice appeared stating that a two-day convention would be held at the Wesleyan Chapel in Seneca Falls, New York. The purpose of the meeting was "to discuss the social, civil, and religious condition and rights of women."

The first women's rights convention, organized by such pioneers in the struggle as Elizabeth Cady Stanton and Lucretia Mott, brought together three hundred men and women to vote on a "Declaration of Sentiments" based on America's Declaration of Independence. The convention also approved a controversial resolution that it was "the duty of the women of the country to secure to themselves their sacred rights to the elective franchise," a right held at that time by no woman in the world.

The women and men who gathered at Seneca Falls were the front lines of a movement that sought to change the way women were treated in the United States. In nineteenth-century American society, females were second-class citizens whose proper place, many thought, was to be in the home obeying the commands of their husbands and taking care of their children.

Life as a housewife in the 1840s involved such backbreaking work as hauling water from a well for household use; ironing clothes during the hottest weather with heavy, metal irons; and scrubbing dirty clothes on a washboard using harsh lye soap. Each meal had to be made from scratch as there were no prepackaged foods available to be picked up from the local grocery store.

10

For American housewives in the nineteenth century, such day-to-day chores as cooking and washing often involved backbreaking work with little relief from hot weather.

INDIANA HISTORICAL SOCIETY, MARY LYON TAYLOR COLLECTION (2)

Although in 1848 women in New York had been given the right to the property they owned before marriage, most women in the country did not have this right, nor the legal custody of their children, nor the right to the property or earnings they acquired after marriage. "The power of a husband," noted women's historian Aileen S. Kraditor, "legally extended even to the right to prescribe the medicine his family must take and the amount and kind of food they ate."

At four years old, Mary Eliza Wright was too young to attend the Seneca Falls meeting, but she would spend her life fighting to see that women were treated as equals with men. Born on May 27, 1844, in Greenfield, Milwaukee County, Wisconsin, Mary Eliza was the second daughter and youngest of four children of Philander Montague and Mary Weeks Wright.

The girl's parents were originally both from New England and had moved to Ohio, where they met and married. Friends knew Mary, the mother, as a "sweet and charming" person with a perfect taste in books. Philander had been a schoolteacher before becoming a farmer. The Wrights lived on a forty-two-acre farm described by a family member as "homely and plain and storm beat and scarred by many a stain."

Mary Eliza, who adopted the name May for herself, proved to be a bright child, receiving instruction from her father and from schools in Wauwatosa and Bloomington, Wisconsin. Remembering her early days in Wisconsin, she said she inherited from her family a "passion for human liberty in all its phases," as well as the knowledge that men and women were not treated equally in America.

Family legend has it that Philander Wright wished for his daughter to follow in his footsteps and attend Harvard University. He told May that she had the right to receive a quality education and the ability to find work in a job for which her talents suited her.

There were, however, limited opportunities for women in higher education in nineteenth-century America. Even those who wanted women to have advanced schooling sometimes did so only in the belief that the knowledge might improve their ability to be housewives and mothers, and female students often studied sewing and painting instead of mathematics and history.

Luckily for May, her father supported her attempts to become educated. In 1863, in order to pay for her additional schooling, she took a teaching job in Waukesha County, Wisconsin. One-room schools modeled after those of New England dominated the state's educational system during the time May taught there. Housed in simple buildings (a Wisconsin historian noted that a school was considered advanced "if it had separate toilets for boys and girls") and equipped with limited

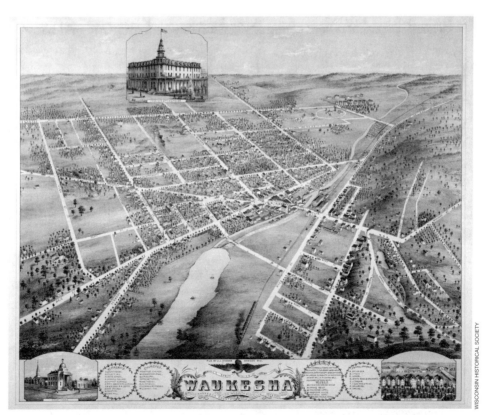

WISCONSIN HISTORICAL SOCIETY

An 1874 bird's-eye view map of Waukesha, Waukesha County, Wisconsin.

supplies, schools were led by teachers with little or no training.

To secure a job as a teacher, a person needed only an eighth-grade education. A superintendent responsible for hiring teachers in one state even went so far as to claim that a teacher who could neither read nor write might be "best for a school of beginners." Like May, many teachers in Wisconsin—and throughout the country in the late nineteenth century—were young women, poorly paid, who started in the profession at age eighteen or nineteen. It was not uncommon in these country schools for a few of the students to be older than the teacher.

There were a few high points in May's early days as a teacher. In a letter to a friend she rejoiced at the delivery of a real blackboard for her class. Although used and not in the best condition, it proved a better

WISCONSIN HISTORICAL SOCIETY

A teacher poses with her class before a one-room schoolhouse in Wisconsin. The school is similar to the one May Wright Sewall worked at while a teacher in Waukesha County, Wisconsin.

teaching tool than what she had used before: wooden boards painted black.

Working all day and studying at night took its toll on the young teacher, who complained to a friend: "I am so tired that if I could only rest free from labor, care & anxiety for a few years & then be resurrected, why perhaps I might enjoy life some. And what good is my work & worry to accomplish after all? If I were to kill myself in the service of the little pests (whom for all their indifference, I can't help but loving) not one of them would 'rise up and call me blessed.'"

In the fall of 1865 May left teaching to study at an institution that tried to offer women an education equal to that given to men at such celebrated universities as Harvard and Yale: the Northwestern Female College in Evanston, Illinois. She was drawn to the school, founded in 1855 by the brothers William P. and Colonel J. Wesley Jones, in part because a friend of hers had studied there.

Before the Jones brothers established their college, there were very few institutions of higher education open to women in the Midwest. The new college, said J. Wesley Jones, would try to provide young women plenty of opportunities for a thorough college education "near home and amid such rural seclusion as will secure every possible guaranty [*sic*] for health, morals, and refinement."

In spite of financial difficulties and a fire that destroyed the college's first building, the Northwestern Female College had grown by the time May entered the school into a respected place for women's education. Students from all over the country flocked to its campus.

Her one year at Northwestern became for May a time of serious study of such subjects as chemistry, Latin, zoology, logic, and trigonometry. "In those days," she later observed of her college career, "I was a very unsociable person, absorbed in books and caring little for any other manifestation of the human spirit, so almost everyone knew more about

COURTESY NORTHWESTERN UNIVERSITY ARCHIVES (2)

Students gather in front of one of the few buildings at the Northwestern Female College in Evanston, Illinois. William P. Jones and his brother founded the college with the stated goal of offering to "Young Ladies of the Northwest" a "thorough Collegiate Education near home, and amid such rural seclusion as will secure every possible guaranty [sic] for health, morals, and refinement."

the 'come and go' of the daily life of the college than I." May said she was
disappointed that her classmates were not "more brilliant, more exacting
of themselves and of me," and also believed that her teachers were more
kind than talented.

In 1866 May and six other women received their diplomas from the
Northwestern Female College. The next summer, she returned to her
teaching career at a school in Grant County, Wisconsin. May found a job
as a teacher in Cody's Mills (today Corinth), Michigan, before moving on
to Plainwell in 1869 to serve as teacher and principal at the town's high
school.

While in Plainwell May met Edwin W. Thompson, a mathematics
teacher from Paw Paw, Michigan. She described Thompson—after
making him shave off his mustache—as "gentle in manners, and nature" as
well as having "a fine literary taste." May left Michigan in the fall of 1871
for a new assignment—teaching German at the high school in Franklin,
Indiana, for $60 per month.

On March 2, 1872, May returned to Michigan to marry Edwin.
The young couple returned to Franklin in 1873, with Edwin taking over
as superintendent and May becoming principal of the high school. The
newlyweds worked in a city that had just undergone a boom in education.
A new high school, called "one of the best school buildings" in the state
by one historian, had been opened in February 1871, and its former
superintendent H. H. Boyce had established the city's first graded school
system.

Both May and Edwin were pleased with their new home. "Our
present position," she wrote a friend back in Wisconsin, "is in every
respect preferable to Plainwell. It [Franklin] is three times as large, and
our salary is correspondingly generous; besides, success here means much
more than success in a town of Plainwell's size; and if we are to be teachers
we have the American desire to be prominently successful ones."

The couple only stayed in Franklin for one year, however, before resigning to accept positions in Indianapolis—May as an instructor in German and later English, and Edwin as a teacher in the business department at Indianapolis High School. The couple joined a staff of a school that like many in the state had had a rocky start, but would grow into one of the finest educational institutions in Indiana.

When the Thompsons first moved to Indianapolis, they lived in rooms at a house on North New Jersey Street, just off Fort Wayne Avenue, and later moved to a residence at 273 Christian Avenue. The couple soon became part of one of the city's most intellectually active neighborhoods: an Indianapolis subdivision known as College Corner.

The neighborhood's pleasant atmosphere was also improved through an organization that offered its members a social and educational service during a time when few entertainment activities were available. In the fall of 1872 two Indianapolis schoolteachers organized the College Corner Club, a literary society with membership open to both men and women drawn mainly from the area. May and her husband joined the group,

A view of Shortridge High School, formerly known as Indianapolis High School, where May Wright Sewall taught.

whose meetings were known for "free discussion, literary flavor and social charm," and also included some original work by club members.

Through their association with the College Corner Club, and shared membership in an early suffrage society (the Indianapolis Woman Suffrage Society, formed in April 1873) and in the local Unitarian church, a group of women in the neighborhood formed an organization that continues as the longest running of its kind in the state: the Indianapolis Woman's Club. The club held its initial meeting on the frigid afternoon of February 18, 1875.

The Indianapolis gathering did not mark the first time that women in America, or Indiana, had formed such a group. In 1858 Constance Fauntleroy returned to New Harmony, Indiana, after living in Europe. In August and September 1859, Fauntleroy, joined by other women, met in the Old Fauntleroy Home to discuss the possibility of forming a woman's club. On September 20, 1859, the women formed a reading and literary group called the Minerva Society, whose object was "the mental improvement of its members."

In spite of Fauntleroy's pioneering efforts in Indiana, the first models for women's clubs are generally credited to the New England Woman's Club, formed by Caroline Severance and Julia Ward Howe, and the group Sorosis, organized in 1868 by women who were unhappy about being denied attendance at a New York Press Club dinner for famed British author Charles Dickens. "We have proposed," the women announced in establishing Sorosis, "to enter our protest against an idle gossip, against all demoralizing waste of time, against the follies and tyrannies of fashion, in short, against anything that opposes the full development and use of the faculties conferred upon us by our Creator."

In Indianapolis, most opposed any changes in the way women led their lives as homemakers. "The air was thick with prejudice against woman escaping from her sphere," noted Martha Nicholson McKay, an early organizer of the Indianapolis Woman's Club.

McKay discovered that there were some in the community who expressed doubts about joining the new women's group. One woman wrote McKay that she found her mission in life in taking care of her two children, and did not wish to do anything else. Another "well-meaning woman," McKay added, wrote expressing her belief that McKay should be able to "see that your God-given duties point in another direction."

In order to win over these doubters, McKay tried to assure women that the group did not intend to form a suffrage society or involve itself in the temperance crusade. Years later she noted that the club came into being out of a "sincere desire" to help women bring together their life in the home and outside cultural opportunities.

McKay managed to convince six other women to join her in her home's parlor, a "pleasant room" decorated in typical Victorian style with a walnut glass-door bookcase, a walnut secretary along each side of the mantel, a sofa, a rocking chair, and chairs upholstered in black haircloth. A plaster statue of Dickens looked down upon the meeting as McKay was joined by her mother, Jane Nicholson, and five other women, including May, to form the new organization.

The club's original constitution called for the group to be an "organized center for mental and social culture" for its members—a statement later changed to include the phrase "and for the improvement of domestic life." To achieve this goal, the association encouraged a "liberal interchange of thoughts by written essays and discussions upon all subjects pertaining to its objects."

The Indianapolis club's second meeting, held a week after its first, saw the election of Eliza Hendricks, the wife of Indiana governor Thomas A. Hendricks, as president; May became chairman of the club's executive committee. To meet the goals stated in its constitution, the club assigned as the subject for discussion at its next meeting the following: "To be a

19

good housekeeper, is it needful to devote one's entire time to the work?"

Although the housekeeping topic seemed to be a safe one, the group endured some rough moments in its early history. Its first president, Hendricks, did not bother to attend meetings. A history of the club speculates that Hendricks may have kept away from the club because she feared that it "might turn out to be a suffrage society in sheep's clothing," and she was already more interested in public affairs than literary matters. The Hendricks incident highlighted one of the group's problems: how could it balance the needs and desires of its more liberal, women's rights-related members, with more conservative women?

"Lest our little craft should sink in an uncharted sea," noted McKay, "the first programs were designed to quiet the fears of the anxious." These programs included such seemingly ordinary matters as the advantage of selecting Tuesday instead of Monday for wash day, and hints on how to clean silver. The more conservative club members, said McKay, herself a suffragist, were "appeased by papers on the newest discoveries in domestic science, or the always fruitful theme of how best to govern children."

By the end of its first decade the club, which met on the first and third Fridays of every month and limited membership to a hundred people, found itself doing fewer programs on cooking and cleaning and sponsoring more talks on such subjects as English and French history. In fact, everything became a topic for debate, except for such forbidden areas of discussion as politics and religion.

Encouraged by the group's success, club members were not bashful about sharing its success with others, even those who believed that a woman belonged in the home. Speaking enthusiastically about the club to a rabbi who happened to be visiting the city, McKay received the response that his wife's place was "in her tent [at home]." The veteran clubwoman merrily replied: "Oh yes, we know that. We only want her to have a window in it."

INDIANA PICTURE COLLECTION, MANUSCRIPT SECTION, INDIANA STATE LIBRARY

Grace Julian Clarke became a good friend of May's and later worked to win Hoosier women the right to vote through her work with the Woman's Franchise League.

Organizations such as the Indianapolis Woman's Club served to train future leaders in community affairs and in the national battle to win for women the right to vote. The Indianapolis Woman's Club produced such community organizers and suffrage advocates as May and McKay, as well as such future club leaders and feminists as Grace Julian Clarke, president of the Indiana Federation of Clubs and an officer for the Woman's Franchise League.

In the summer of 1875 May left Indianapolis to join her husband at Mountain Sanitarium in Asheville, North Carolina. Edwin had contracted tuberculosis and had gone to North Carolina in hopes that the mountain climate might offer him some relief from his illness. Unfortunately, he could not regain his health, dying on August 19, 1875. His last request to his wife, reported the *Indianapolis Evening News*, was that "the worn out body be left among the hills."

In a resolution honoring Thompson, the Indianapolis school board proclaimed that in him they "recognized a scholar of large attainments, remarkable for his clear and vigorous mind, a successful instructor, a kind and sympathetic friend, a genial and cheerful companion."

Her husband's death caused May to attempt to always live up to his excellent character. "My husband had the purest, strongest and tenderest spirit I have ever known," she wrote a friend. "*To be with him was* my supreme joy, and now that he is gone from me, to *grow up* to the *stature* of his spirit is my one object." She lost herself in her work, returning to her classroom at Indianapolis High School. But just a few years after her loss, May discovered a cause that would consume her energies for some time to come: gaining for women the right to vote.

Chapter 3

The Suffragist

During the spring of 1878 Indianapolis society crackled with "mysterious whisperings" concerning a proposed meeting involving women in the community with "advanced ideas" about their proper place in society. A secret call drew ten people—nine women and one man—to a gathering at Circle Hall.

Although the issue of improved rights for women had been seriously debated in Indiana as far back as the 1850s, most respectable citizens opposed such ideas as radical. "Had we convened consciously to plot the ruin of our domestic life, which opponents predict as the result of woman's enfranchisement, we could not have looked more guilty or have moved about with more unnatural stealth," said May Thompson, one of those who attended the meeting.

The conservative atmosphere that dominated Indianapolis could be seen from the group's taking more than two hours to discuss whether or not the new society should take a name for itself that would clearly state its goal, or one that would hide it from the outside world. About a month after this initial meeting, twenty-six people attended a second gathering, this time at the home of Zerelda Wallace. At the meeting, those attending agreed to form the Indianapolis Equal Suffrage Society. The society consisted of men and women "willing to labor for the attainment of equal rights at the ballot-box for all citizens on the same conditions."

During the next seven years, the society campaigned for its cause by holding forty-three public meetings, distributing thousands of pamphlets, and sponsoring talks by such nationally known suffrage figures as Frances Willard, Susan B. Anthony, and Elizabeth Cady Stanton.

Through its various parties and other activities, including literary exercises, the society, noted May, "became a factor in the social life of the city" and became the means by which the association secured for itself "greater popular favor" than it could have gained otherwise.

May's work with the local association gained her admission into such national women's suffrage groups as Anthony and Stanton's National Woman Suffrage Association (NWSA), where she served as one of Anthony's "most competent young lieutenants." Just a few months after its birth, the Indianapolis society selected May as its representative to the NWSA's thirtieth anniversary convention held in Rochester, New York.

In the first of her many appearances on the national stage, May, who gave a report on efforts in Indiana to secure voting rights for women, won praise from Stanton, Anthony, and civil rights leader and former slave Frederick Douglass. Suffragist Lucretia Mott praised the Indianapolis teacher's "strength, philosophic clearness and beauty of diction." As Anthony biographer and fellow Hoosier Ida Husted Harper noted, May became a close friend to Anthony and one of the many "valuable workers to the cause of woman suffrage" joining the fight during the decade from 1870 to 1880.

In fighting for women's rights in the nineteenth state, May followed a path blazed by such early pioneers as New Harmony's Frances Wright and Robert Dale Owen, who fought in the Indiana Constitutional Convention of 1850–51 to include in the new state constitution the right for a woman to own property.

The nineteenth state's early property laws, noted one Indiana historian, were based upon an English legal tradition that viewed women "as perpetual juveniles." Owen, given a testimonial dinner for his efforts by Hoosier women following the convention, wrote Anthony that

LIBRARY OF CONGRESS

Suffragists Susan B. Anthony (right) and Elizabeth Cady Stanton formed a unique partnership over the years in their struggle for women's rights. Of their partnership, Stanton noted that Anthony "supplied the facts and statistics, I the philosophy and rhetoric, and together we have made arguments that have stood unshaken by the storms of . . . long years; arguments that no man has answered."

although he campaigned for property rights for women while in the legislature, he did nothing in regard to suffrage. During those days, Owen said, such a goal would have been impossible to achieve.

Owen knew what he was talking about. Many of his fellow delegates at the constitutional convention were horrified by his attempts to improve property rights for women. One delegate claimed that if the convention adopted Owen's measure "it would be to throw a whole population morally and politically into confusion. Is it necessary to explode a volcano under the foundation of the family union?" Another delegate said that he opposed Owen's proposition "not because I love justice less, but woman more."

Even women who supported Owen's efforts on their behalf when it came to property rights were very careful to avoid such dangerous ground as seeking full political rights with men. In a letter distributed to the state's newspapers calling for a memorial to Owen, Sarah T. Bolton and Priscilla Drake emphasized that they were demanding only "protection for the property that Providence may enable us to give our daughters," and downplayed "the efforts of those of our sex who desire to enter the political arena—to contend with men at the ballot box, or sit in our public councils."

There were some in Indiana, however, bold enough to consider the shocking notion that a woman should be allowed to vote. At an antislavery meeting in Greensboro, Indiana, in 1851, Amanda Way,

Robert Dale Owen, son of the founder of New Harmony, Robert Owen, and a respected reformer, diplomat, and politician, pushed for women's rights in the Hoosier State while serving in the Indiana General Assembly.

INDIANA HISTORICAL SOCIETY, BASS PHOTO COMPANY COLLECTION

a licensed minister, offered a resolution declaring that women were "being oppressed and degraded by the laws and customs of our country," and were treated as little better than slaves.

To help women in Indiana, Way called for holding a women's rights convention. In October 1851 at Dublin, Indiana, a group of women met for a "full, free, and candid discussion of the legal and social position of women," she noted.

A report on the "thrilling meeting" printed in William Lloyd Garrison's *The Liberator,* a weekly newspaper firmly opposed to slavery, and written by Henry C. Wright of New Garden, Ohio, reported that much talk centered on whether or not women's roles as mother, wife, daughter, and sister might be harmed if they voted or ran for public office. "It was in answer that if voting and holding office would degrade women," Wright said, "they would degrade men also; whatever is injurious to the moral nature, delicacy, and refinement of woman is equally so to man."

A year after the Dublin meeting, the Indiana Woman's Rights Association was formed during a convention in Richmond. Elected as the group's vice president, Way insisted that unless women demanded their political, social, and economic rights—including the right to vote—they would continue "in the future, as in the past, to be classed with Negroes, criminals, insane persons, idiots, and infants."

In 1859 the association presented a petition to the Indiana General Assembly, signed by a thousand men and women, seeking for women not only the same property rights as men, but also asking that the state constitution be amended "so as to extend to woman the right of suffrage." The legislature accepted the petition and passed it on to a committee, which, to no one's surprise, decided that the time was not yet right to give Hoosier women such rights.

After these early gains, which included the first woman speaker to appear before the state legislature, the women's rights movement in

Indiana came to a standstill due to an overriding national emergency: the Civil War. The Woman's Rights Association held no meetings from 1859 to 1869, a time when suffragists were giving their time, labor, money, and even lives "to the cause of freedom for the country."

The association was reborn after the war as the Indiana Woman's Suffrage Association and sponsored its first meeting in ten years, from June 8 to 9, 1869, at Indianapolis's Masonic Hall. The gathering received positive notices from the *Indianapolis Journal*, which noted that the assembly "compared favorably with the best that have ever been conducted by our own sex." The rival *Indianapolis Sentinel*, however, claimed in an editorial that "no amount of human ingenuity can change the arrangement of nature. When woman ceases to be womanly, woman's rights associations become her fitting province."

The resurgence of the Indiana women's suffrage organization came at a time when national leaders in the fight were split on the issue of the Fifteenth Amendment to the U.S. Constitution. The amendment prohibited states from denying voting rights to people based on their race, color, or previous condition of servitude. Disagreements on this and other issues led to a splitting of the ranks into two national organizations.

Led by Anthony and Stanton, the NWSA focused its energies on winning women the right to vote through the action of the federal government. The less radical American Woman Suffrage Association (AWSA), guided by Lucy Stone and Henry Ward

Sarah T. Bolton won early fame in Indiana as a poet, especially for her work "Paddle Your Own Canoe." In addition, she advocated property rights for fellow Hoosier women.

INDIANA HISTORICAL SOCIETY

Beecher, concentrated on a state-by-state effort, often working at the city and state levels to win voting rights for women in school board and other municipal elections as a way to finally achieve full suffrage rights for women across the country.

This national split caused some problems in state organizations, including those in Indiana. At its annual meeting in 1870, the Indiana Woman's Suffrage Association narrowly agreed to become an auxiliary of the NWSA. The Hoosier group, however, did call for a union of the NWSA and AWSA "as soon as practical." To head off any difficulties, the Indianapolis Equal Suffrage Society, according to May, held itself "aloof from all formal alliances." This gave the group the freedom to work with any individual or organization that had as its aim giving women the right to vote.

May's work on behalf of women's rights was helped a great deal by the total support of one man—her second husband, Theodore Lovett Sewall. Born in Ohio, Sewall had been raised in Wilmington, Delaware, where he attended Taylor and Jackson's Scientific, Classical and Commercial Academy. A member of a distinguished Massachusetts family, Theodore, at age sixteen, entered Harvard College, becoming the seventh member of his family to receive his education from that famous college. He graduated in 1874, ranking fifth in a class of 158.

The young man impressed Harvard president Charles Elliott, who described Sewall as "a person of irreproachable character, excellent ability and good address." In 1876 Elliott recommended Sewall to a group of prominent Indianapolis citizens who were seeking a person to serve as head of a school for boys in the city.

Sewall opened the Indianapolis Classical School with only nine students on September 25, 1876, in a room located in an old building of the North Western Christian University at the corner of Home and College avenues. The school soon won favor from the community for

Preamble and Constitution of The Woman's Rights
Association of Indiana.

Whereas: The subject of Woman's Rights is founded upon the
eternal rock of Truth, and as unceasing and untiring
activity is absolutely necessary for the promulgation
of information regarding Woman's condition, needs
and claims; and as united action and permanent
organization, further the cause most efficiently — we
whose names are hereunto subscribed, unite together
under the following Constitution:

Art 1st — This Society shall be known by the name of the
Indiana Woman's Rights Association.

Art 2nd — The officers of this Society, shall consist of
President, Vice President, Corresponding & Recording
Secretary, and Treasurer
whose duties shall be such as devolve upon
such stations and they shall be elected annually

Art 3rd — The Secretary further, shall be requested to
report annually upon the general condition
of women, and the efforts made for her elevation

Art 4th — Persons shall be appointed at each annual
meeting to report upon each of the following
subjects; "Woman's Labor and Remuneration,
"Woman's Legal condition" — "Woman's social
Position" and "Woman's Education".

Art 5th — This Society shall meet annually at such
time and place as shall hereafter be determined
upon.

Art 6th — This society does advise the organizing of
District Societies throughout the State.

Art 7th — All persons attending the meetings of this
Society shall have full privilege, and shall
be desired to take part in the deliberations
but the right of voting is reserved to the members

Stricken out by the Society

Art 8th — This constitution may be altered or amended
at any regular meeting of the Society.

Lydia W. Vandenburg Richmond   Mary F. Thomas
Mary B. Birdsall.   "   Jno Owen Thomas
Minerva Maulsby, Economy   Elda A. Smith.   Pendleton

INDIANA HISTORICAL SOCIETY, BV2577

*The Preamble and Constitution of the Indiana Woman's Rights
Association founded in 1851.*

its difficult courses. The school's aim, Sewall said in an announcement about its opening, would be "to give boys a thorough drill in Latin, Greek, Arithmetic, Algebra, Geometry and the elements of the modern languages and physical science; in short, to serve as a Preparatory School for the best Eastern Colleges," all for just $100 per year.

By the opening of the 1878–79 term, the school had four teachers and approximately sixty students. From one small room, the school had grown to occupy an entire floor in the old university building. A reporter noted that the new rooms were "pleasant, well furnished, adorned with maps and pictures, and admirably adapted for school use; and finally, that from its location the school will attract scholars from a large section of the country."

As head of a thriving school, Sewall became a respected figure in the community, even winning membership in the exclusive Indianapolis Literary Club, a men-only organization. Grace Julian Clarke, a friend of both May and Theodore, remembered one of the couple's first meetings at a Unitarian church service. "Mr. Sewall had recently come from Boston, a Harvard graduate, a type of the modern Puritan in appearance, retiring in manner but with a pleasant frank smile," Clarke said. "I recall seeing him go forward to meet her as she approached, he looking very tall and slim in a Prince Albert coat and silk hat, and she radiant in a brown silk dress . . . and a bonnet tied under her chin with a pink ribbon."

Theodore and May were married on October 31, 1880. In his work at the school, Theodore had the assistance of a strong group of teachers, including his wife, who resigned from her teaching job at Indianapolis High School to join the boys' school staff as a German teacher for the 1880–81 school year. She later taught a class in English literature.

In marrying again, May found a perfect partner for her advanced views on the educational, occupational, and political status of women. "Marriage is the natural condition," May once told a reporter, "but I believe in woman living her own life and working out her own salvation in her own way." Reflecting on her marriage to Theodore, May told Clarke she was thankful "to have a husband whose tastes and ideals were in entire sympathy with her own."

The steady, level-headed Theodore and his reform-minded wife made a perfect team. They shared the same interests, including a love of books and reading, and he encouraged and aided his wife in all her work. The couple's togetherness impressed their friends. Clarke recalled seeing the Sewalls at the public library before the start of their first trip to Europe, sitting together at a table "with a mountain of books before them, he calling her attention to certain things and she nodding."

Old friends of the couple noted that Theodore served as a "'balance wheel' to his energetic, enthusiastic, but sometimes impractical wife." In the years to come the Sewalls' equal partnership became well known in suffrage circles. Alice Stone Blackwell, daughter of suffragist Lucy Stone and one of the editors for the *Woman's Journal*, wrote May in 1897 noting that the newspaper would be featuring a series of articles on husbands of distinguished American women. She asked May to contribute an article about her husband. "You know that there is a popular belief that the husbands of suffragists do not amount to anything," Blackwell wrote. "We want to show the fallacy of this by writing up the husbands, especially those who really have amounted to something."

With her husband firmly committed to her cause, May became a leader in the fight to secure voting rights for women in Indiana. According to May, the problem in the nineteenth state came not from it being a lost cause, but from overconfidence. She wrote Sarah Andrews Spencer, corresponding secretary for the NWSA, that Hoosier women believed suffrage was "so *sure* a thing that it is not necessary to struggle for it."

In December 1880 the Indianapolis society issued a letter, signed

COURTESY ROBERT W. SEWALL

33

Images of Theodore L. Sewall as a student at Harvard and as head of the Indianapolis Classical School.

by Wallace as president and May as secretary, to each legislator and to leading newspapers in the state indicating that during the next session of the Indiana General Assembly the group would seek action on the suffrage question.

The Indiana General Assembly opened its business in January 1881 with Republicans and Democrats equally split in the House and the Republican Party controlling the Senate. Governor Albert G. Porter, a Republican, warned legislators that during the session women would ask to be heard regarding an amendment to the state constitution granting women the right to vote.

In fact, said May, the suffragists were determined to attack the issue in two ways. One was to seek passage of a bill that would "immediately authorize women to vote for presidential electors." The second involved approval of an amendment to the state constitution allowing women to vote in all elections. May said that if the electoral bill passed, it seemed certain legislators would go on to approve passage of the constitutional amendment as well.

Although the presidential elector bill, introduced by Marion County representative John W. Furnas, passed two readings in the House, it fell three votes short of making it past a third reading. The defeat came in spite of emotional pleas on the bill's behalf by suffrage supporters Mary Haggart and Helen Gougar, who had first suggested that her fellow reformers seek a legal opinion on whether women—even though they were barred from voting in state elections—might still be allowed to vote for presidential electors.

Failure in one area, however, did not mean total defeat for the suffragists. The regular legislative session had ended before lawmakers had the opportunity to act on important state matters. Therefore, the legislators had to remain in Indianapolis for a special session from March 8 to April 16. The special session gave Indiana women the opportunity to pursue their second route for winning the right to vote: amending article two, section two of the state constitution to give women the vote in all elections.

On March 15 Furnas introduced a resolution in the House outlining a constitutional amendment giving Hoosier women the right to vote. The resolution passed the House and, one day later, the Senate followed suit by approving the resolution. In addition to the suffrage amendment, the legislature—responding to a petition signed by 46,000 voters—also approved a constitutional provision prohibiting the manufacture and sale of alcohol.

Immediately after the passage of the suffrage bill, the Indiana

INDIANA HISTORICAL SOCIETY, BASS PHOTO COMPANY COLLECTION

View of the Indiana Statehouse at the time legislators argued the merits of allowing women to vote in the nineteenth state.

TIPPECANOE COUNTY HISTORICAL ASSOCIATION

Lafayette's Helen Gougar proved to be a staunch ally of rights for women in Indiana. In addition to her work on behalf of suffrage Gougar worked in journalism.

Woman's Suffrage Association and the Indianapolis Equal Suffrage Society invited all legislators who had voted for the amendment to a party to celebrate this achievement on behalf of woman's rights. May noted that the defeat of the presidential elector effort had helped pave the way for the state constitutional amendment victory. "No one believed that the bill to amend the constitution would have passed," she said, "had it not been preceded by the battle over the electoral bill and the consequent education of the General Assembly in regard to this great question of political rights."

The battle for woman's suffrage in Indiana, however, was far from over. According to the terms of Indiana's constitution, any amendment to it had to be passed by two consecutive legislatures and then sent on to Hoosier voters for their approval. Recognizing the difficult road ahead, the Indianapolis suffrage group worked feverishly over the next few years to attract supporters to its cause.

Hoping to have an Indiana legislature filled with members willing to repass the suffrage amendment in 1883, both the state and Indianapolis suffrage groups sponsored meetings and lecture tours, and helped organize local suffrage societies. In the spring of 1882, the state association called for a mass meeting of all Hoosier women interested in having the suffrage amendment approved. Those who could not attend were asked by the group to send a postcard indicating their support; the association stopped counting after receiving five thousand postcards in response.

May, who presided over the meeting held on May 19 at Indianapolis's Grand Opera House, had nothing but praise for those who attended. "If any came to scoff," she noted, "they remained to participate with pride in this remarkable convention." At the time, she added, the meeting was often "referred to as the largest and most impressive" ever held in Indianapolis.

That summer women spoke at political meetings and attended state conventions as delegates. Suffrage supporters traveled all over the state to speak on behalf of their cause in front of Sunday school meetings, teacher associations, agricultural fairs, picnics, and assemblies of all kinds.

May believed woman's suffrage should have received support from Republicans and Democrats. "It is included," she said, "in the fundamental principles of both parties." Although she admitted that there were probably more Republicans than Democrats who believed in woman's suffrage, she argued it was unnecessary, and unfortunate, if it was made a partisan issue. "There are Democrats as well as Republicans among women," she noted, "and women do not wish to be bound to any party by having their cause espoused by a party as a party."

Unfortunately for May and her fellow suffragists, a woman's right to vote did become a bitter political issue. At its August 9 convention in Indianapolis, the state GOP approved a resolution demanding that the suffrage amendment and the other amendments passed by the 1881 legislature be adopted and passed along for a decision by Indiana voters. "These amendments were not partisan in their origin," the Republican party noted, "and are not so in character, and should not be made so in voting upon them."

Indiana suffragists, however, still faced an uphill battle, thanks, in part, to firm opposition to the prohibition amendment from both the Democratic Party and the liquor industry. A week before the GOP convention, the Democrats had gathered in Indianapolis and indicated the party's strong stand against the prohibition amendment, and used its opposition to temperance as a campaign issue.

Businesses that manufactured liquor did all they could to oppose the prohibition amendment, and also worked against the suffrage amendment. One historian noted that these firms worked against giving women the right to vote because they feared if such a situation occurred, women would have enough power to successfully pass laws banning the manufacture and sale of alcohol. Even May said that the interests of both suffrage and prohibition in the 1882 campaign were identical. It came as no surprise then, that these groups attracted the opposition of the liquor industry, she noted.

The election proved to be a disaster for both suffrage and temperance supporters, with the Democrats winning control of both the House and Senate. With the Democratic sweep, May said, the suffragists had "no grounds for hoping that the amendments would be re-passed and sent on to the voters of the state for final adoption or rejection."

The constitutional amendments, including the suffrage and temperance measures, did not die without a fight. When the Indiana General Assembly opened for business in January 1883, the suffragists could at least count on the support of recently elected Wayne County senator William Dudley Foulke, a firm supporter of a woman's right to vote and a temperance advocate. "The demand for woman's suffrage was really the demand for woman's liberty," said Foulke.

Foulke submitted a resolution to the legislature on behalf of the Indianapolis Equal Suffrage Society. The organization called upon the lawmakers to "submit to the qualified voters of the State, at a special election, an amendment to the Constitution of the State, giving to all its citizens, without distinction of sex, the right of suffrage." The society also asked the legislature to approve a resolution requesting Congress to vote for a federal amendment to the Constitution giving women the right to vote.

Instead of risking a direct vote against the suffrage and temperance amendments, Democrats hit upon a better plan. Democratic lawmakers argued that all the proposed constitutional amendments, which seemed to have been approved by the previous legislature, had in fact not been legally adopted because they had not been properly entered in the journals of either the House of Representatives or Senate. A majority report from the senate judiciary committee claimed that there was no evidence in the journals to indicate that either of the houses of the legislature "referred, or intended to refer, a proposition to amend the Constitution to this Assembly."

Republican state representative Christian Holler tried again to secure suffrage for Hoosier women by successfully introducing a resolution on the issue in the House of Representatives on February 20. Although the resolution was adopted by a 53 to 42 vote, the Senate refused to act on the resolution.

A frustrated Foulke complained that lawmakers during the session had failed to approve "a single measure of importance to the state." He doubted if Indiana, in its entire history, could provide "an illustration of a legislature so utterly useless . . . as the general assembly of 1883."

May and her colleagues were "disappointed" by the legislative defeat, "but not discouraged." She claimed that the local suffrage society continued to "labor with undiminished zeal" and sought every opportunity to prove that women could be a factor in state politics.

Moving her efforts to the national stage, May was one of the speakers at NWSA's sixteenth annual convention in Washington, D.C. In her talk on March 6, May claimed it was not "a grander thing to lead the forlorn hope in 1776, not a grander thing to strike the shackles from the black slaves in 1863, than it would be in 1884 to carry a presidential campaign on the basis of 'Political Equality to Women.'" The next day May appeared before a U.S. Senate committee and told the senators woman's suffrage was a "just measure," not a partisan one, due to women "by virtue of our heritage and our one father, our one mother eternal."

To match her words with action, May sent a letter to Indiana delegates to the national GOP convention reminding them that there were 70,000 people in the Hoosier State who had petitioned for a woman's right to vote. "We urge you, therefore," the letter stated, "to consider their interests by not voting for any candidate known to be opposed to suffrage for women."

In spite of all her efforts, May and other Hoosier suffragists found their achievements in the 1881 legislature hard to match in the years to come, with the period 1882 to 1900 being "one of uneven activity in Indiana" for woman's suffrage, as one historian noted. Lawmakers friendly to woman's suffrage continued to introduce resolutions and bills in the general assembly, but were always met by firm opposition from those who considered women as second-class citizens.

There were, however, some bright spots for the suffrage cause in Indiana. In May 1887 the Indianapolis society, aided by Anthony, reorganized itself into a state organization allied with the NWSA. The next year the NWSA held its annual convention in Indianapolis. Meeting at Rushville in May 1888, delegates from the Indiana branch of the NWSA and the AWSA agreed to merge into one state organization. Although May received a majority vote at the meeting to remain as an officer of the new organization, she refused for "personal reasons" to serve.

Those personal reasons may have had to do with May's increasing role as a leader in the NWSA (she served as chairman of the organization's executive committee from 1882 to 1890). May used her organizational skills to their utmost from 1887 to 1890 when the two suffrage associations agreed to merge into a new group called the

A journalist and poet, William Dudley Foulke served in the Indiana State Senate from 1882 to 1886. He later became president of the American Woman Suffrage Association.

INDIANA PICTURE COLLECTION, MANUSCRIPT SECTION, INDIANA STATE LIBRARY

National American Woman Suffrage Association.

May also traveled outside the United States to speak on behalf of suffrage for women. On one visit to Canada she even won the respect of an opponent of woman's suffrage, a lawyer from Halifax, Nova Scotia, named J. Murphy. In June 1897 Murphy related to Elbert Hubbard, an American writer who also happened to be a friend of the Sewalls, a debate he had with May. Talking about the debate, Murphy noted that he had accepted the challenge only to avoid giving Canadian suffragists "an opportunity to crow."

With the hall packed with the "finest audience" he ever witnessed in Halifax, Murphy told Hubbard that every person in the crowd must have felt he received his money's worth. "The question remains practically in the same state as it was before the debate commenced," Murphy said. He added that he regarded May as "a very clever woman indeed, and if she was more of a woman and less of a reformer and agitator I suppose my affection would be just a trifle deeper."

In her letters to fellow suffragette Anthony, May often addressed her as "Dear General" and, like a general, Anthony could be hard on her troops. In December 1897 Anthony complained to May about the workload forced upon her by the writing of her biography, which became "like a ball and chain to me," she noted. Anthony went on to warn May that she and other "young folks must not talk of hard times nor the opposition of other work, nor family cares nor anything under the sun but just to push through to the best of your ability."

Although Anthony recognized Sewall's talent for organization, and often called upon her and another trusted lieutenant, Rachel Foster Avery, to plan and execute complex tasks such as the formation of the International Council of Women and other meetings and conferences, she never "strongly considered" May for a high leadership position in either the NWSA or the NAWSA.

A FEMALE SUFFRAGE FANCY.

LIBRARY OF CONGRESS (2)

An 1871 illustration from Frank Leslie's Illustrated Newspaper *(top) shows suffragist Victoria Woodhull making the case for women voting before the Judiciary Committee of the House of Representatives in Washington, D.C., while another (bottom) cartoonist imagines what would happen if women gained suffrage.*

What stopped Anthony from placing her friend in a top post was her realization that woman's suffrage happened to be just one in a series of interests May was involved with during her life. For while she battled to win for women the right to vote in Indiana, May had also been making her mark in Indianapolis with what was a unique community institution for its time: the Girls' Classical School.

Chapter 4

The Girls' School

During the late nineteenth century, Indianapolis experienced a boom in both its population and industry. In spite of this, the city had, as historian and author Claude Bowers noted, "the charm of a large country town."

Bowers remembered his days in the capital city as comfortable ones. Those who lived in the city led quiet lives and "businessmen went home for lunch and in the evening found time . . . to read the [*Indianapolis*] *News* and to stroll across velvety lawns to the neighbors' to exchange views on what they read," he said.

One of the most fashionable avenues in the community was Pennsylvania Street. Mary McLaughlin, who lived in a comfortable home on that street, remembered that maple trees lined the roadway, offering cool shade even on the warmest days. The street was also a place where mule-driven streetcars kindly stopped for passengers in the middle of the block, "as they never seemed to be in a hurry to get downtown," McLaughlin remembered.

Another resident of the neighborhood, Charlotte Cathcart, noted that nearly "everyone came to Pennsylvania street to walk, no matter if they lived on Delaware or Meridian." At twilight the street's residents sprinkled the dirt street with water from hoses, which, McLaughlin said, "cooled everything off and made our evenings on the porch and on the lawn very happy times."

The quiet nights were looked over by a night watchman, an older man equipped with a whistle that he blew when he reached every corner. Safe in her bedroom under the covers on her bed, McLaughlin often wondered if the blast of the whistle in the quiet night might "tell the thieves and robbers where he is."

Although she remembered a number of famous people who frequented the neighborhood, including Benjamin Harrison, elected as president in 1888, and several Indiana governors, McLaughlin in particular recalled a woman whom she often saw "coming up our street, often carrying a large bag of books, and walking briskly along"—May Wright Sewall. It was not surprising that McLaughlin frequently spied May strolling down the sidewalk, as the McLaughlin home on Pennsylvania Street was just one door down from the Girls' Classical

INDIANA HISTORICAL SOCIETY, BASS PHOTO COMPANY COLLECTION

Mule-powered streetcars were a familiar sight on Indianapolis streets when May Wright Sewall lived and taught in the city.

School, which had opened in 1882 and which May ran with her husband, Theodore.

Until its closing in 1907, the school offered Indianapolis's girls an education equal to that found for boys in the Indianapolis Classical School and one based on the entrance requirements established for admission to such nationally known women's colleges as Smith, Vassar, and Wellesley. A college graduate herself, May believed that higher education was "a means to some of the largest and noblest ends, but it is also in itself a noble end."

The Girls' Classical School opened with forty-four students in attendance in September 1882 on the southeast corner of Pennsylvania and Saint Joseph streets. The school, which eventually attracted pupils from across the country, taught its students something different from the usual courses girls had been taking in other schools, including such subjects as painting, drawing, and music.

Earlier schools for women organized in the city, such as the Indianapolis Female School and Miss Hooker's Female School, had concentrated on teaching students how to act like ladies rather than to train their minds for serious study. The Girls' Classical School offered two four-year courses of study, classics and English, with an additional year for pupils preparing for college entrance examinations. The course also included French and German, and the school emphasized that "Music, Painting, Drawing and similar branches" would not be offered.

May served as principal and also taught literature at the school. She took a firm hand in running the operation. "There was no nonsense about Mrs. Sewall," one student remembered. The pupil noted that May used to come into her classroom, and after briefly speaking to the teacher, she talked to the students, all the time looking at them "through a large magnifying glass which enlarged her eye" and transformed her into "a Cyclops of most forbidding appearance."

INDIANA PICTURE COLLECTION, MANUSCRIPT SECTION, INDIANA STATE LIBRARY

The Girls' Classical School in Indianapolis opened in September 1882 on the southeast corner of Pennsylvania and Saint Joseph streets.

Even before the Girls' Classical School opened, May, no stranger to a life of study, had insisted that women were the equals of men when it came to learning. In a column for the *Indianapolis Times*, May quoted a Doctor William Goodell of Philadelphia who reported instances of four cases of mental exhaustion, and one case of insanity, brought about by "over brain-work at school." In fact, the doctor commonly asked women who came to him asking his advice on health matters: "Did you stand high at school?"

May had nothing but contempt for Goodell and other physicians of the time who often advised young girls to drop out of school so as not to harm their health. Nearly every teacher in the country would testify that they have never had a case of a young woman breaking down due to hard study, May wrote. The real problem, she said, came about when teenage girls were faced with the double role of student and society woman. Ultimately, the society role wins out over studying and parents withdraw their daughters from school. "She gradually regains the condition which, in a woman, people are satisfied to call 'health,'" May wrote, "and is henceforth cited as a proof that 'girls cannot endure severe and protracted mental effort.'"

In opening a school with high standards, May, with her husband's support, had given herself, as one Hoosier education historian noted, an ample "opportunity to apply some theories of her own in the education of girls." One of these theories involved physical training for her students, something not usually offered to girls who attended school during the nineteenth century.

This special attention to exercise, including gymnastics under the direction of Richard Pertuch, the physical education teacher at the Boys' Classical School, resulted in another first for the girls' school: a dress code. Theodore might have influenced May's thinking by his attempt in March and September 1881 to institute a standard way of dressing for students in the boys' school. A simple dress code, Theodore believed, would promote "discipline and gentlemanly manners both in and out of school."

Shortly after the girls' school opened, May sent a letter to parents and friends of the institution seeking their opinion on whether or not to adopt a simple school dress for everyday wear, which included a kilt skirt with loose waist and a sash. Such an outfit, she later noted, allowed for freedom of movement, no pressure on any part of the body, no more weight than necessary for warmth, and "quick changeability."

Although May said she would not adopt a dress code "unless the parents are nearly unanimous in its favor; and, if adopted, it will be compulsory upon no one to buy or wear it," she did have some immediate suggestions concerning a particular item: shoes. Those students who wore high heels made it impossible for them to participate in physical exercise, May noted. Whether or not the school dress was adopted, she called on mothers to "see that their daughters wear thick-soled shoes with low and broad heels."

In a catalog for the institution published in May 1883 Theodore noted that early in the school's history "a loose school dress of uniform style was adopted, which has contributed largely to the ease and pleasure of the gymnastic exercises, as well as to the general health of the girls." He also praised the intelligence of the girls enrolled at the school, noting that in both the amount and quality of the work done the pupils "have shown themselves at least equal to the pupils in the School for Boys."

Local newspapers shared Sewall's passion for the mental and physical energy of the students at the Girls' Classical School. Following a gymnastic exhibition at the school on June 2, 1883, under Pertuch's direction that included marching exercises, wand exercises, calisthenics, and other demonstrations, one newspaper account indicated that the exercises "were performed with a grace and ease that quite astonished

INDIANA PICTURE COLLECTION, MANUSCRIPT SECTION, INDIANA STATE LIBRARY

May Wright Sewall (far left) and her husband, Theodore (far right), chaperoned nine students from the Girls' Classical School on a trip to Washington, D.C. Here the group poses in front of Mount Vernon, the home of George Washington.

even the parents of the girls."

After a visit to the school, a reporter from the *Indianapolis News* came away with the opinion that a "spirit of happiness is suffused through the school." The reporter was particularly impressed by the senior class of girls, noting the following: "They are not the kind of girls who lose their temper and self-possession under difficulties. They are not the sort of person who scream at trifles, nor do they call everything 'lovely'— cabbages, waterfalls and all—and they are not the ones who wear shoes a great deal too small when they are young, and require shoes a great deal too large when they are old. They appear permanently well poised, mentally and bodily."

The discipline shown by pupils at the Girls' Classical School came about in no small part from the strict way in which May ran the school. Reminiscing about their former school, students—the daughters of Indianapolis's leading businessmen and socially prominent mothers— described May as "a bit of a tyrant," whose stern look could strike terror in their young hearts.

During school hours, students maintained a strict study schedule, with set hours for subjects such as reading, geography, writing, spelling, arithmetic, foreign languages, gymnastics, and grammar. Known for her promptness, May expected the same behavior from her students, often reminding them that school started at 8:30 a.m., and not a minute later. To those who claimed they did not have the time to work out a problem or translate a sentence, May always replied: "You mean you did not budget your time—you had all the time there was. You wasted it."

May also offered advice to parents on how students should act outside of the classroom. In a letter sent to parents she noted that the hours of 2 p.m. to 4 p.m. should be set aside as a time for students to relax, but only in a certain way. She warned parents not to let their daughters waste their free time by visiting friends, shopping, or attending society parties.

LIBRARY OF CONGRESS

Students at the Girls' Classical School had the opportunity to meet some of the leading figures of the time, including Susan B. Anthony.

May's strict standards could, however, be too much on occasion, even for someone as sure of herself as famed suffragist Susan B. Anthony. Once while visiting May in Indianapolis to discuss suffrage matters, Anthony also toured the girls' school. Writing about the visit in her diary, Anthony noted: "Mrs. Sewall introduced me to the girls of her Classical School as one who has dared [to] live up to her highest dream. I did not say a word for fear it might not be the right one."

So many students wanted to attend the school that in August 1884 the Sewalls announced they would open a new building at 426 North Pennsylvania, which included a new primary department admitting both

For the 1886–87 school year, the Sewalls leased a double brick building at 343 and 345 North Pennsylvania Street for use as a residence for those attending the Girls' Classical School.

INDIANA HISTORICAL SOCIETY, BASS PHOTO COMPANY COLLECTION

girls and boys at age six. The three-story brick building, dominated by a tower rising above the main roof, included two session rooms capable of seating sixty students, two session rooms with seating for thirty pupils each, four classrooms, an office, and a gymnasium.

By the 1886–87 school year, the Sewalls had leased a double brick building at 343 and 345 North Pennsylvania for use as a residence for those attending the school from outside the city. M. F. Sproule, formerly with the state institution for the blind, became the woman in charge of maintaining order at the girls' residence, and May spent every Friday evening leading residents in "general conversations on practical and literary themes."

In addition to their work at the school, the Sewalls worked hard to turn their home (first on New Jersey Street and later at 343 North Pennsylvania Street) into the literary and cultural center of Indianapolis.

Every Wednesday the Sewalls sponsored discussions in their drawing room, described as "a blue and terra-cotta retreat that can be extended to the magnificent length of seventy feet." There anywhere from one hundred to two hundred people gathered to debate the issues of the day. "No invitations are issued for these affairs," noted a reporter who profiled May for a leading American magazine, "for it is intended than any one, irrespective of bank accounts, may air his opinion or ride a pet hobby."

For these occasions May could also be counted upon to brew tea for those assembled, and made bread and preserves that were the envy of other Indianapolis housewives. Guests particularly enjoyed May's lettuce sandwiches, made with crisp lettuce on thin slices of bread that were spread with mayonnaise with lemon seasoning. Julia Moore, who served as May's secretary, described her employer as being "a remarkable housekeeper and a wonderful cook."

The Sewalls' guest room also served as a temporary shelter for the numerous visitors entertained by the couple over the years. Visitors ranged from suffragists such as Anthony, Frances Willard, Ida Husted Harper, Anna Shaw, and Lucy Stone, to writers Hamlin Garland, Elbert Hubbard, and Booth Tarkington, to even traveling actors such as Otis Skinner. Skinner described May as "a woman of rare culture, highly intellectual and vitally interested in the higher education of women," and noted that she always made theater people welcome in her home.

Those who enjoyed the Sewalls' hospitality were asked to sign a register noting their stay, but were asked to put no personal compliments in the book. "Friends disobeying this command," the couple warned, "will not be invited again to sleep under our roof." Most visitors, however, cheerfully ignored the Sewalls' warning against flattery and filled the register with their thanks and good wishes.

As well as serving as a social center for Indiana's capital city,

Hoosier artists T. C. Steele (left) and William Forsyth (right) helped pave the way for the creation of the Art Association of Indianapolis.

the Sewalls' home also became a launching ground for a number of organizations that made their mark on the community, including three groups still in existence today: the Art Association of Indianapolis (today known as the Herron School of Art and the Indianapolis Museum of Art); the Propylaeum, home to a number of women's organizations; and the Contemporary Club, a literary group open to both men and women. Although busy with the affairs of the Girls' Classical School and her commitments to woman's suffrage, May still found time to play a key role in starting each of these Indianapolis institutions.

In the case of the art association, it started with a lecture. In the winter of 1881 May invited Nancy H. Adsit of Milwaukee to Indianapolis to give a series of illustrated lectures on ceramics. Adsit's visit produced a positive enough reaction that she returned two years later for another art lecture, this time covering engraving and etching. At the lecture's end, Sewall asked those present who were interested to meet at her home to discuss the possibility of organizing a society to study and promote art.

Such a task had been accomplished before in Indianapolis. In 1877 the Indianapolis Art Association had been established to display the work of such well-known local artists as Jacob Cox and T. C. Steele, but the group disbanded after only one exhibition. Also that year James Farrington Gookins and John Washington Love, both foreign-trained artists, opened the Indiana School of Art. Although the school only lasted for two years, its pupils—including future Hoosier Group member William Forsyth—refused to give up on their work and formed the Bohe Club.

May's proposal, she noted, received "a cordial response," and in early March 1883 a committee of ten people was selected to write a constitution for the group. After holding ten "hard-working meetings," as May noted, the committee produced a constitution adopted at a public meeting at the Denison Hotel on May 7, 1883. The group formally incorporated itself that October with Albert E. Fletcher as president and May as recording secretary.

From its creation the Art Association of Indianapolis had intended to have an equal number of men and women in its membership, but found that women dominated its board of directors in its early years. May had an explanation for this: "In a relatively new community, largely devoted to manufacturing and commercial interests, the number of men in whom taste and leisure for official service in such an organization . . . is small."

The association had as its goal the advancement of art in all its forms, including art instruction and lectures on the subject. Also, realizing that "the art instinct 'grows by what it feeds upon,' and that people can learn to love art and to distinguish between the good and bad in it only by seeing what is good," May said, the association worked as well to sponsor regular art exhibitions.

For assistance in organizing its first exhibition, the association turned to Sue M. Ketcham, a local artist. To find paintings for the exhibition, Ketcham traveled to Chicago, Detroit, and New York, eventually gathering 453 paintings representing the work of 137 artists.

The art association held its first exhibition from November 7 to 29, 1883, in a room at the English Hotel. The display, one local historian noted, "was a decided success," with attendance "increasing steadily to the last." From the exhibition, the association purchased two paintings—Harry Chase's *Running for an Anchorage* and Percival DeLuce's *The Anxious Mother*—as the first items for its permanent collection.

Encouraged by the exhibition's success, the association two months later opened an art school with Ketcham and Charles F. McDonald of the Chicago Art League as teachers. May, along with Anna Dunlop and Henry S. Fraser, worked to manage the school's business affairs, but their efforts failed.

The minutes for the association for this period, said May, were "very gloomy reading; the teachers were efficient and devoted, the business management hopeful and untiring; but without proper quarters, without endowment, without material, the school could not be maintained longer; and the year following its close special entertainments were given under the auspices of the board to liquidate the debts incurred by the school."

With the burden of debt from the school hanging over its head, the association did not organize an arts exhibition in 1884, but sponsored a display the following year. The association's exhibition featured work from a group of Indiana painters, including Steele and Forsyth, who had been studying in Munich, Germany.

The association's exhibition became an annual event and an important date on the community's cultural calendar. In addition to the annual exhibition, which over a twelve-year period displayed more than four thousand paintings, the association sponsored other displays highlighting such works as etchings, engravings, pottery, carvings, tapestries, fabrics, embroideries, and architectural drawings. Also during that same period the association offered six courses of lectures, translating into twenty-four separate talks.

During all this time the association operated without a permanent headquarters. Monthly board meetings were held at private residences and meetings involving the membership were usually held at a local hotel. Thanks to May's intelligence and the devoted work of other women in the community, however, the association and other organizations in Indianapolis soon had a building designed for their activities: the Propylaeum, whose name means "gateway to higher culture."

The Propylaeum had its beginnings in a trip May made to her former home, Milwaukee. While in the city she delivered a talk before the local woman's club, which had built the Milwaukee Athenaeum through the formation of a stock company. Inspired by their example May, upon returning to Indianapolis, related her plans to her husband and secretary, Moore, during dinner.

Moore later recalled that May told her and Theodore: "I thought all the way on the train of a plan for the Indianapolis women. We can build and operate a Club House right here, we could sell stock enough to build it, could locate it centrally . . . and we can make money, for all the clubs will rent of us, the Woman's Club will have a definite home instead of wandering from one Church parlor to another, and it will eventually become a centre of culture for the city."

On April 30, 1888, the Indianapolis Woman's Club appointed a committee of seven women, including May, to find the organization a suitable room in which to hold its meetings. May, who served as chairman, shocked others on the committee by boldly stating the group should at once reorganize itself to consider "the feasibility of forming, among the women of Indianapolis, a stock company for the purpose of erecting and owning a building which should be specially adapted for the use of the various clubs, literary, artistic, and social, which are so numerous among us."

May later said that she was inspired to suggest such a venture by the work of other women who had successfully constructed buildings, including the Milwaukee Athenaeum; the Ladies' Library Association of Kalamazoo, Michigan; and the Woman's Club of Grand Rapids, Michigan.

The members of the Indianapolis Woman's Club committee had serious doubts about such an effort, questioning whether such a scheme would be possible and wondering whether or not enough women could be found to make such a project work. Displaying her usual force of character, May calmed the committee's fears by firmly exclaiming: "Ladies, this thing will be done. If you do not take hold of it others will."

On June 6 the committee incorporated itself as the Indianapolis

Propylaeum and issued $15,000 in stock. It also limited the purchase of stock to women only. The Propylaeum did not want to exclude men from the project, one committee member noted, but wanted "the pleasure of saying to our husbands, brothers and sons, our building is at your service, as yours have always been at ours; come often and enjoy it with us."

Sixteen days after its incorporation, the Indianapolis Propylaeum offered shares of stock at $25 each to other women in the community. Thirteen women took advantage of the opportunity to become involved in the project, and in addition a board of directors was selected numbering fifteen people.

A committee responsible for finding a site for the building looked for a central location with easy access by streetcars, yet at the same time "removed from the noise and bustle of business." For a cost of $5,500, the committee found such a place at 17 East North Street.

With a site chosen, the Propylaeum board appointed a seven-member committee, which included May, to oversee construction. Plans for the building included a dining room and large kitchen, two parlors capable of seating two hundred people, and a second floor assembly room with room for six hundred people. The committee hired the local architectural firm of Scherrer and Moore and spent more than a year discussing and studying plans for the building.

In May 1889 the Propylaeum's board recommended to its stockholders an increase in the capital stock from $15,000 to $20,000. The stockholders agreed to the change, and by March 10, 1890, all of the stock had been sold. Funds from the sale were enough to hire a contractor, Jungclaus and Schumacher, and the cornerstone for the building was laid in a ceremony held on May 8, 1890.

The only problem during the cornerstone ceremony occurred when Doctor Joseph S. Jenckes, former pastor of Saint Paul's Episcopal Church, who led the ceremony, threw a nickel into the hollow cornerstone. A young boy darted out of the crowd, grabbed the nickel, and ran. Jenckes immediately took off after the troublemaker, the tails of his black coat flying behind him as he ran. The minister managed to overtake the boy, take back the coin, and replace it in the cornerstone.

The Indianapolis women's high hopes for the Propylaeum were almost dashed by a simple fact: the group did not have enough money to construct the building it wanted. May broke the bad news to stockholders at the group's second annual meeting just four days after the cornerstone had been laid. Acting to secure the necessary funds for completing the project, the stockholders authorized the board of directors to borrow up to $10,000, an amount the group managed to obtain from the Crown

The original Propylaeum building in Indianapolis was located on the south side of North Street, between Meridian and Pennsylvania streets.

Hill Association, the group responsible for operating a local cemetery.

With the financial crisis averted, the board appointed a three-member committee, which included May, to supervise construction. Those involved with the project were impressed by May's dedication to the project, noting that she made daily visits to the site and "watched every brick, stone and board as it was placed in position."

The Propylaeum was formally dedicated on the evening of January 27, 1891. The eight hundred people gathered for the ceremony included stockholders and guests, presidents of the city's clubs, Indiana governor Alvin P. Hovey, Indianapolis mayor Thomas Sullivan, and representatives from the three women's organizations previously cited by May as serving as the inspiration for the efforts to construct the Propylaeum.

In her presidential address, May made some clever digs at the male sex, noting that in her work seeing to the building's construction she found the average man, "as charmingly unconscious of the value of time in the matter of engagements, and as bewitchingly incapable of regulating his movements by the clock and the calendar as any woman living."

Turning to more serious matters, she said the Propylaeum would serve the community as a portal, giving men and women opportunities for meeting at the highest intellectual level, and sharing between the two the "hospitalities of thought as well as those of the table." Over time, the building would come to be "the center of all those influences which make for culture."

Just two days after its dedication, the Propylaeum hosted its first club, the Matinee Musicale, which presented a program and reception. Other organizations quickly followed suit, including the Indianapolis Literary Club, the Portfolio Club, the Dramatic Club, the Art Association, the Indianapolis Woman's Club, and a group organized at the Sewalls' home just six months before the Propylaeum opened—the Contemporary Club of Indianapolis.

Members of the Indianapolis Woman's Club gather for the group's last meeting at the original Propylaeum on March 16, 1923. Razed as part of the construction for the Indiana War Memorial Plaza, the Propylaeum found a new home at 1410 North Delaware Street in Indianapolis.

The Contemporary Club provided something unavailable in the city at that time: membership open to men and women on equal terms with "no excluded subjects, no forbidden ground," said May, who served as the organization's first president. She noted that prior to the club's formation, the only chance women in the city had to meet men on equal terms to discuss ideas came at the Indianapolis Literary Club's ladies night.

The club held its first meeting on September 25, 1890. Through the years the club, which still meets today, heard talks by such noted speakers as historian John Clark Ridpath, writer Garland, artist Steele, politician William Dudley Foulke, and reformer Jane Addams.

Not everyone in Indianapolis approved of May's work, as some were offended by her visibility, influence, and sometimes dominating personality. McLaughlin, the Sewalls' neighbor, recalled that as a young girl she was out walking with her mother when the two met May, who stopped to talk to them as she often did. McLaughlin noted that her mother always defended Sewall. Perhaps knowing of her friends' dedication, Sewall once unburdened her frustrations on McLaughlin's mother, lamenting: "I cannot walk down this street without being misunderstood."

In the early 1890s May had bigger problems than the occasional harsh words of enemies when she learned that Theodore had contracted tuberculosis—the same disease that had killed her first husband. Because of his illness, Theodore had to give up his teaching and other duties at the Girls' Classical School, as his doctor advised him to travel to New Mexico to improve his health. As May continued to worry about her husband in the spring of 1895, she received news of an unexpected gift that would help the work of the Art Association of Indianapolis.

On Monday morning, May 13, May received a visit at the Girls' Classical School from Ambrose P. Stanton, a local attorney and her friend for the past twenty years. His first words to her were: "You are the president of the art association, I believe." Agreeing that she was, May responded: "And you have come to bring a fortune."

An astonished Stanton informed May that John Herron, who had worked in real estate and lived in Indianapolis for fourteen years before moving to California, had recently died in a fire in Los Angeles.

In his will, Herron had left the bulk of his fortune, approximately $225,000, to the art association to establish and maintain an art school and gallery named in his honor. "Mr. Herron had long wanted to endow some kind of an institution," said Stanton, who served as executor of Herron's will. "He was not an expert in his scrutiny of art, but loved to look at pictures and selected the Indianapolis Art Association as the beneficiary of his money."

On May 25 the officers of the art association held a public meeting at the Grand Opera House to share the news of the Herron bequest and, as May noted, to see if "other citizens might be stimulated by Mr. Herron's example to become in a noble sense promoters of art in this community." The association's joy turned to worry, however, as a group of Herron's distant relatives contested the will. Also, as May observed, the association had to deal with both attorneys and legislators "who thought to make either fees or political capital out of abetting the contestants of the will."

Already upset by the battle over the Herron bequest, May faced a much greater tragedy when Theodore died at their home early in the morning on December 23, 1895. The respected Indianapolis educator had returned to Indianapolis shortly after Thanksgiving after a stay in a sanitarium in Poughkeepsie, New York. "A few days after his return," the *Indianapolis News* said in its obituary on Theodore, "he became so much worse that he was forced to take to his bed, and he continued to sink."

In his last message passed on to the students of the school he started with his wife, he said: "Tell the girls that to be well and to be at work are the two conditions of happiness."

Theodore's death meant, as one friend of the couple noted, "the desolation of one of the happiest, most perfect homes ever made by two mortals." A shocked May sent a telegram to her friend Anthony with the simple statement: "Dear General, my Theodore is taken." Anthony replied, telling May to "be brave in this inevitable hour; take unto yourself the 'joy of sorrow' that you did all in mortal power for his restoration, that his happiness was the desire of your life; find comfort in the blessed memories of his tender and never-failing love and care for you in all these beautiful years."

May was so overcome by her husband's death that she was unable to attend a memorial meeting held in Theodore's honor on January 6, 1896, by the members of the Girls' Classical School and its alumnae association. Ella Laura Malott, an 1891 graduate of the school, remembered that when students failed to reach the high standards set by Theodore, they could feel "his silent disappointment" and vowed to try harder next time. When pupils did meet his high standards, Malott said they were "rewarded by his silent look of approval. His silence then expressed more to us than countless words of praise."

Theodore's death caused many in the community to question whether the Girls' Classical School could survive. To put a stop to rumors that the school might be sold, May sent a letter to parents and alumnae indicating the gossip "has not now, nor has it ever had, the slightest foundation." Her husband's death, she went on to say, made her more determined than ever "to do my utmost to mature and execute the plans we had made for the continuance and permanence of the school."

Even without her husband's steady hand and strong support, May, as principal of the Girls' Classical School, continued to expand the institution's offerings, including offering adult education classes and starting a new Department of Industrial Domestic Science with courses in chemistry and physics as well as cooking. She also remained active in civic affairs, particularly with the art association.

In October 1897 the association disposed of claims from Herron's relatives challenging his bequest. Finally, in March 1899, a committee appointed by the association, which included as members May, Stanton, and C. E. Hollenbeck, devised a plan for dividing the Herron bequest into three funds: $150,000 for the art treasure fund, $10,000 for the art school fund, and $65,000 for a building and grounds fund.

From April 1899 to January 1900 the association considered a number of sites in the city for an art building before finally deciding to purchase for $50,000 the Talbott property, also known as the Tinker

House, at Sixteenth and Pennsylvania streets. The association occupied the property on February 11, 1902, and a month later the John Herron Art Institute was formally opened to the public.

Three years later, after much arguing about cost and location, May had the honor of digging the first spadeful of dirt for the association's new museum and art school, designed by the Indianapolis firm of Vonnegut and Bohn. On November 25, 1905, the association laid the cornerstone for its new structure. It was an important moment for the association, but May noted that the public did not share in the group's enthusiasm for the project.

Expecting a large crowd to attend both the cornerstone ceremony and a public program preceding the event at Mayflower Church, the association board had secured a large force of police to help with crowd control. "The result was that twelve solemn gentlemen in uniform guard the wraps of the three ladies bearing a part in the program rendered at the church," said May, "and afterward served to swell to apparent dignity the little body of faithful members who acted as the president's bodyguard while she used the trowel."

Success with the art association came at a time when May had money problems with the Girls' Classical School. In 1903 she confided to Anthony that she had experienced some "sad disappointments in regard to the non return of some pupils none of them, however, because of dissatisfaction with the school, but I am relying upon unexpected accessions to balance counts."

The drop in student enrollment came about from increased competition from the city school system, and from a former teacher at Sewall's school, Fredonia Allen, who in 1902 had started a rival institution, Tudor Hall School for Girls (today known as Park Tudor School).

In May 1905 May announced that she had entered into a partnership

INDIANA HISTORICAL SOCIETY, BASS PHOTO COMPANY COLLECTION

The Art Association of Indianapolis selected the Talbott property (also known as the Tinker House) at Sixteenth and Pennsylvania streets to become the first home of the John Herron Art Institute.

to run the Girls' Classical School with Anna F. Weaver, a former student at the school and a graduate of Stanford University. May informed friends and patrons of the school that Weaver would share with her "all the responsibilities, financial as well as executive, and in every way having equal authority and equal responsibility."

The partnership continued for two years, but by late February 1907, May decided to retire and sell the school to Weaver, who moved operations into the double residence on North Pennsylvania Street. May sold the school building to the College of Musical Art for $20,500. Weaver continued to run the school until 1910, when it closed for good.

In a letter May sent to graduates of the school informing them of her intention to retire at the end of the school year in June, she noted that an entry in her diary made the night before the school opened in 1882 said the following: "To-morrow I commence a work to which I now expect to give the chief part of my life for twenty-five years." Working with her students over the years had "resulted in advancing my own education. I hope that I have not been the only one profited by my efforts, but that you also feel it is good for you and that it *will continue* to be good for you to have had and to continue to have this intimate relation with my life."

May's retirement from the girls' school was front-page news in Indianapolis newspapers. The *Indianapolis News* reported that the educator did not know what she might do in the future, but had received "several offers in literary and lecture fields."

With her retirement, May also began donating to various institutions in the city the numerous books, articles, and artwork she had collected over the years. She gave the local library three hundred books; a number of reports, pamphlets, and magazines; and programs from clubs from throughout the United States and around the world. The art association received May's collection of Mexican pottery and art catalogs from galleries she visited on her travels.

By clearing her home of these items, May was saying farewell to a community she had served since she had come to teach at Indianapolis High School in 1874. She left Indianapolis in the summer of 1907 to give lectures at Green-Acre-on-the-Piscataqua in Eliot, Maine. Established by Sarah Jane Farmer in 1892, Green Acre held conferences each summer on various aspects of religion and philosophy that featured such nationally known speakers as Edward Everett Hale, W. E. B. DuBois, Booker T. Washington, John Greenleaf Whittier, and William Dean Howells.

Even before she had left Indiana for Maine, however, May and her genius for organization had won fame far beyond the borders of the nineteenth state through her work with two groups: the National Council of Women and the International Council of Women.

Chapter 5

The Council Idea

Throughout her very active life, May Wright Sewall received many thanks for her efforts on behalf of women everywhere. Nothing, however, matched the reception she received in Prague (today the capital city of the Czech Republic) during a visit she made there in 1916.

When her train from Berlin pulled into Prague's station, Sewall was amazed to see a large crowd ready to welcome her to the city. As she stepped from the train, local officials gave her a richly illustrated manuscript in the Czech language, and she was taken to the community's council chambers to address the city. The crowds were so great at the hall that the head of the city government could not make his way through to give his welcoming speech. "It was," Sewall later said of the event, "the most beautiful, the sweetest and the most romantic experience of my life."

The Indiana educator and suffragist achieved international fame through her pioneering efforts on behalf of the "council idea." To Sewall, the main point of her idea was harmony. She wanted to bring together women with different interests so that they could see how much they actually had in common and how they could work together to accomplish "a common unselfish purpose."

Sewall's idea grew into a plan for a National Council of Women for the United States as well as countries throughout the world, and eventually a permanent International Council of Women composed of national councils.

Using her genius for getting things done, Sewall, who served as president of the International Council of Women from 1899 to 1904, won the honor of being called by a popular American magazine of the day as the leader of five million women in eleven countries.

The grand plans for an international union of women began with the work of Sewall's two old suffragist allies—Susan B. Anthony and Elizabeth Cady Stanton. In 1882 Stanton visited England and France and, after discussions with "distinguished publicists and reformers of different countries," decided to create an international woman's suffrage association.

During the next year Stanton, joined by Anthony, discussed the idea with suffragists in England. At a reception held in their honor in November before returning home to America, Stanton and Anthony presented their idea to friends of woman's suffrage gathered at the reception. Those attending the reception passed a resolution stating that the "time has come when women all over the world should unite in the just demand for their political enfranchisement."

The movement for an international suffrage association, however, struggled to gain ground for four years with only a few letters of "mutual encouragement" passed back and forth across the Atlantic Ocean. All that changed, however, at the National Woman Suffrage Association's nineteenth annual convention in 1887, where plans were made to celebrate the fortieth anniversary of the 1848 Seneca Falls meeting by holding an International Council of Women in Washington, D.C., in 1888.

At the NWSA convention, however, the ideas of pioneer suffragists such as Stanton and Anthony clashed with the views of a younger generation of women represented in part by Sewall. "Many of the older women . . . at first desired the proposed international meeting to be limited to the advocacy of equal political rights," she noted. According to Sewall, younger women wanted to expand the meeting to include all sorts

LIBRARY OF CONGRESS

May Wright Sewall during her days as president of the
International Council of Women.

of women's groups.

To help achieve that goal, Sewall introduced a resolution calling for a meeting of an International Council of Women "to which women workers in all lines of social, intellectual, moral or civil progress and reform shall be invited, whether they be advocates of the ballot or opposed to woman suffrage." Anthony and other older suffragists modified the resolution to read that the meeting, to be sponsored by the NWSA, would include "all associations of women in the trades, professions and moral reforms, as well as those advocating the political emancipation of women."

The difficult task of planning and preparing for the meeting fell to the NWSA's executive committee, but most of the work was put upon the shoulders of Sewall, Anthony, and Rachel Foster Avery. The first task undertaken by this suffragist trio involved writing an invitation calling on women to attend the meeting.

In writing the invitation, the three women had many disagreements, with most of the complaints coming from Sewall. After receiving one fourteen-page letter of suggestions from Sewall, Anthony wrote Avery in late April 1887 expressing her frustration over the executive committee's failure to come to an agreement. "Sewall thinks she had everything all right . . . but none of the rest of us think with her," Anthony said.

Just a month later, however, Anthony's frustration with Sewall had turned to respect at the Hoosier's dedication to the cause. "Sewall is just as full of work every minute as ever—it tires one to see her go—but then she has everything so perfectly systematized . . . that she accomplished everything just as she plans," Anthony wrote Avery. "She is a marvel as to executive ability."

By June 1887 the NWSA executive committee had finally agreed on an invitation for the international meeting to be held at Albaugh's Opera House in Washington, D.C. The committee had high hopes for the gathering, noting that exchanging opinions on the great questions of the day "will rouse women to new thought, will intensify their love of liberty and will give them a realizing sense of the power of combination."

Although the invitation claimed that women throughout the world had been ignored and rejected by men in power, it went on to say discussion at the meeting would not be limited only to "questions touching the political rights of women." Instead, groups invited to attend would include "literary clubs, art unions, temperance unions, labor leagues, missionary, peace and moral purity societies, charitable, professional, educational and industrial associations."

With the invitation for the meeting completed, Sewall and Foster, under Anthony's watchful eye, turned their attentions to corresponding with women's organizations. Sewall collected a list of groups in the United States, while Foster, who had traveled overseas on behalf of the suffrage cause, secured a similar list in foreign countries.

In contacting approximately one hundred women's organizations in America, Sewall discovered "a timidity in accepting an invitation from a suffrage society as well as other limitations." From her experience with these different groups, she developed her council idea, uniting women "on the most democratic basis for the largest interests." Sewall had shared her plans with other suffragists, including fellow Hoosier Ida Husted Harper.

Later, when there was confusion about who should have the credit for creating both the national and international councils, Harper wrote Sewall the following: "I remember distinctly a long talk I had with you in the library of your home in Indianapolis in 1887. You then outlined to me in full detail the plan of a National and an International Council of Women, which should be formed at the International Council that was to meet in Washington in March, 1888, and you said they would far exceed in scope any organization of women in existence."

The effort put forth by Sewall, Avery, and Anthony resulted in a great success. When Anthony opened the meeting in March 1888 forty-nine delegates were on hand representing England, France, Denmark, Norway, Finland, India, Canada, and the United States. Also, fifty-three different national organizations of women were represented. When the council opened on the morning of March 25, delegates filed into an auditorium "fragrant with evergreens and flowers, brilliant with rich furniture, [and] crowded with distinguished women."

Although speakers discussed such topics as education, temperance, legal and political conditions, and professions, the highlight of the meeting came when Sewall laid out the details of her council idea. At the request of Anthony, Sewall briefly discussed her idea of forming two permanent organizations, national and international.

Sewall asked the group to appoint a committee to consider the question. A fifteen-member group—including Sewall, Avery, Clara Barton, and Frances Willard—met and wrote a constitution reflecting the ideas outlined by Sewall. Delegates to the meeting approved a constitution for the National Council of Women of the United States on March 31.

The constitution stated that the women of the United States were coming together "in a confederation of workers committed to the overthrow of all forms of ignorance and injustice, and to the application of the Golden Rule to society, custom and law." The group promised that no club who agreed to be involved with the organization would in any way give up its own work.

In addition, the delegates passed a constitution for an International Council of Women. Officers for the national council included Willard as president and Sewall as corresponding secretary, while Millicent Garrett Fawcett was appointed as president of the international council. Willard and Sewall agreed that their work should at first concentrate on making sure that national councils would be formed in other countries.

To accomplish that goal, Sewall traveled to Europe in the summer

Rachel Foster Avery (right) served as corresponding secretary of the National American Woman Suffrage Association and worked with Susan B. Anthony (below, left) and Sewall to make the first meeting of the International Council of Women a success.

LIBRARY OF CONGRESS (2)

of 1889 to meet with Fawcett and to discuss her council idea at an International Congress of Women in Paris. Although Fawcett had earlier indicated her willingness to organize a council in Great Britain, she refused to follow through on the work. One historian of the women's movement perceived a "clash of temperaments" between the American and British suffragists.

According to Sewall, Fawcett gave several reasons for her refusal to assume the presidency and organize a council in England, including her busy schedule and the time not yet being "ripe" for bringing together the country's women's organizations. Sewall also quoted Fawcett as saying it was "quite impossible that English and American women should have anything in common, the conditions of their lives and the purposes of their respective societies being so different."

Encountering resistance in England, Sewall had better luck in Paris, where she outlined her council idea to a foreign audience for the first time. In her speech to the exposition, she encouraged French women to organize their own council. The object of such a group, Sewall said, would be to bring all women's organizations into a federation and provide for regular gatherings. "In these meetings," she told the crowd, "every cause or object represented by the National organizations which have joined the federation will be discussed by its advocates, and its progress will be officially reported."

After Paris, Sewall continued to speak on behalf of the council idea in Switzerland, giving talks at meetings in Geneva and Zurich and handing out invitations to local women's groups having the same objectives to form national societies that could then become eligible for membership in the National Council of Women (the national groups could then join the International Council of Women).

Sewall's dream of a national confederation of local and state clubs did come true, but not in the way in which she had imagined. In January 1889 at the regular business meeting of Sorosis, usually considered the first organized woman's club in America, Jennie Cunningham Croly proposed that the organization celebrate its upcoming twenty-first anniversary by sponsoring a convention of clubs from around the country.

Delegates meeting at Madison Square Garden in New York two months later laid the foundation for a new organization: the General Federation of Women's Clubs (GFWC). Ella Dietz Clymer, Sorosis president, predicted that the GFWC would "stand related to clubs throughout this land, and, eventually throughout the world, as a great mother to her children—inspiring and controlling by the forces of wisdom and love."

Sewall attended the meeting as a delegate and served on a committee to draft a constitution for the new organization. She also worked hard to recruit clubs in Indiana, Ohio, and Kentucky to join the GFWC, sending personal letters to thirty-six clubs in the three states.

In April 1890 delegates ratified the GFWC's constitution and elected two of the constitution's five authors as its top officials— Charlotte Brown as president and Sewall as vice president. All seemed to be going according to Sewall's wishes, but the group proved to be more independent than she had bargained for. The federation, which considered itself an independent organization, declined to join the National Council of Women.

In spite of her setback with the GFWC, Sewall continued to work to achieve her treasured council idea. When the National Council of Women held its first meeting in February 1891, the organization's membership included a large number of women's groups. During its meeting, the council approved ambitious plans, including urging the National Divorce Reform League to place women on its board; appointing a committee to suggest a business costume for women to "meet the demands of health, comfort and good taste"; and asking the

America's leading women's rights supporters gathered in Washington, D.C., from March 25 to April 1, 1888, for the first International Council of Women. The group included May Wright Sewall (second from right, second row), Elizabeth Cady Stanton (fourth from right, front row), Susan B. Anthony (third from left, front row), and Zerelda Wallace (second from left, front row).

NEBRASKA STATE HISTORICAL SOCIETY

82

Sewall (front row, center) poses with Rachel Foster Avery (left) and other officers of the National Council of Women of the United States.

LIBRARY OF CONGRESS

federal government to pay its employees equal pay for equal work.

Noting that the four hundredth anniversary of Christopher Columbus's discovery of the New World would be celebrated at a World's Exposition in Chicago in 1893, the national council decided to hold the first meeting of the international council in Chicago.

The exposition seemed to be the perfect place for such a gathering. In addition to appropriating funds for the celebration, the U.S. Congress had also approved an amendment by Illinois representative William Springer to a bill creating a national commission to coordinate the fair.

Springer's amendment established a Board of Lady Managers "to perform such duties as may be prescribed by said Commission." Chicago socialite Bertha H. Palmer was selected to serve as president of the Board of Lady Managers, and she invited the National Council of Women to hold its international meeting in Chicago. She promised to make available to the group "the assembly room in the Woman's building, and should that not prove large enough, from our Congress Auxiliary, the magnificent auditorium can be secured for the meetings of the International Council of Women."

To obtain the necessary cooperation from international groups to make the Chicago exposition a success, Sewall, who had taken over for Willard as president of the National Council of Women, once again traveled to Europe to campaign on behalf of her council idea. In 1891 she visited France, Switzerland, Italy, Belgium, and Germany.

In addition to her work overseas, Sewall had been working to convince Charles C. Bonney, president of the World's Congress Auxiliary, which was responsible for sponsoring congresses at the fair to consider "great themes," to adopt the first International Council of Women meeting as one of those official congresses.

Sewall noted that it took a number of letters and meetings before Bonney agreed to the proposal, with the understanding that the meeting's scope should be "enlarged to the greatest possible extent," and it should take the name the World's Congress of Representative Women.

Working once again with Avery, who had been named by Bonney to act as corresponding secretary for the women's congress organizing committee, Sewall continued to campaign on behalf of the international council with women in Europe. Meanwhile, Avery worked to collect lists of national organizations of women that existed in all countries, and to make sure they participated in the upcoming congress.

Between September 1892 and May 1893, Sewall and Avery's organizing committee distributed 7,198 letters and another 55,000 printed documents to women in Austria, the Netherlands, Portugal, Spain, Poland, Mexico, Argentina, Peru, Brazil, Guatemala, China, Japan, Iceland, New Zealand, India, Syria, and Turkey. Impressed by these efforts, Anthony wrote Sewall: "The suffrage work has missed you, oh, so much, still I would not have had you do differently. I glory in Rachel's and your work this year beyond words."

Sewall's grand hopes for the women's congress and her devotion to the two new women's councils, however, placed her in conflict with two influential Chicago women: Palmer, president of the Board of Lady Managers at the fair and president of the woman's branch of the World's Congress Auxiliary, and Ellen Henrotin, vice president of the auxiliary's woman's branch.

Both Palmer and Henrotin not only viewed Sewall as a "radical feminist," but also saw her as using the congress as a way to promote the two councils she championed. Palmer and Henrotin's suspicions about Sewall were increased in September 1892 when they learned of a letter she had sent to Mary Logan, a leader of the Woman's Relief Corps. In the letter, printed on national council stationery, Sewall informed Logan that it was "a most auspicious time for a National Organization to enter the Council," as the national council had "really been given charge of the

INDIANA PICTURE COLLECTION, MANUSCRIPT SECTION, INDIANA STATE LIBRARY

International Council of Women officers gather at the organization's June 1904 meeting in Berlin. May Wright Sewall, wearing an impressive hat, is seated in the front row, fourth from the left. Susan B. Anthony is seated immediately to Sewall's right.

LIBRARY OF CONGRESS

Sewall appears at the San Francisco Exposition in 1915 with a group of other suffrage supporters. Those pictured are: (Front row, left to right) Sewall and Kate Waller Barrett; (Back row, left to right) Anita Whitney, Mary Bear, Vivian Pierce, and Margaret Whittemore.

World's Congress."

As officers of the congress auxiliary, Palmer and Henrotin resented Sewall's claim that the National Council of Women was running the congress, and also feared that women's organizations and clubs might believe they had to join the national council if they wanted to participate in the congress.

Palmer warned Sewall that her attempts to take control of the congress "make no new allies, and no new friends. Your friends will of course stand by you, but those who are doubtful will hold aloof." Palmer also told Sewall that from then on she was to forward all official letters and replies to her in Chicago.

The struggle for control of the World's Congress of Representative Women took its toll on Sewall, who at one point threatened to resign. The storm passed, however, thanks in no little part to the soothing words offered by Sewall's friend and fellow suffragist Avery.

Writing to Sewall from her home in Philadelphia, Avery reiterated her respect for Sewall and her faith in her actions. She went on to write: "It is *because* I feel so well assured of our mutual confidence that I dare to say that . . . I would willingly sacrifice for you and for myself everything except self-respect rather than retire from the positions which we voluntarily entered upon. *Nothing* could repay either of us should we allow any personal feeling to make us leave this Congress in the hands of the people to whom we know its conduct would fall were we to resign."

Sewall stayed on in her position and was able to witness, when the congress met, the coming together of 126 women's organizations from around the world. During the week, eighty-one sessions were held featuring 333 speakers, with as many as eighteen sessions held at one time in different halls. Clarence Young, secretary of the World's Congress Auxiliary, estimated total attendance for the week at approximately one hundred and fifty thousand, and police had to turn away hundreds of people wanting to attend.

The congress marked the first steps toward making the International Council of Women a workable organization. At the Chicago gathering, the ICW met and heard reports about the possible formation of national councils in Canada, France, Finland, and other Scandinavian countries. More important, the ICW elected as its new president Lady Aberdeen (Ishbel Maria Marjoribanks Gordon), a Scottish aristocrat and wife of the governor general of Canada.

Although caught off guard by the honor, Aberdeen accepted the post, one she held almost continuously until 1936. She worked hard to form a national council in Canada. "It was from experience in the Canadian Council," said Aberdeen, "and in watching its development through a chain of local councils between the Atlantic and Pacific, that I began to understand this idea of bringing together diverse people to work for common causes."

With the ICW firmly established, Sewall turned her attention toward an issue that came to dominate her life—international peace. For Sewall, the desire of women for peace came from their view of war as "a menace to the whole spirit of the home, a menace to the children born and reared within the home." The only war to which a woman could give "her heart is that war whose object it is to slay war and establish peace."

At first, Sewall helped to convince the National Council of Women to work on behalf of peace. Although the matter was discussed at the national council's executive sessions in 1893 and 1894, it wasn't until the group's meeting in Washington, D.C., in March 1895 that the council approved a resolution committing the group to the active promotion of peace. The council also supported the efforts of Czar Nicholas II, the leader of Russia, who had called for a conference to establish a panel for international negotiation to work out problems among nations in Europe.

Sewall's work on behalf of world peace with the national council paved the way for similar efforts with the international council. At the organization's meeting in London in 1899—a meeting at which Sewall became the international council's president—representatives from ten national councils of women gathered and made the "far-reaching decision" to pledge the council's support on negotiating international problems.

Sewall used her role as president of the international council to speak out for such reforms as the elimination of nationalism from school textbooks. The council, Sewall noted, asked each of its affiliated national councils to instruct their committees on peace and arbitration to conduct a "rigid examination of all textbooks on the history of their own country which are being studied in its schools."

In the United States, Sewall encouraged the adoption of textbooks that emphasized how industry developed in the country through "successive tides of immigration." Sewall also encouraged mothers throughout the world to remove from their children's nursery any toys that might glorify war.

Even after her term as international council president ended in 1904, Sewall continued to campaign on behalf of peace through her chairmanship of the council's standing committee on peace and arbitration. She became a familiar presence at national and international peace conferences, always ready to talk to audiences about this important issue.

Sewall's promotion of peace continued even with the outbreak of World War I in Europe in 1914. On a visit to Italy in June 1914 she received a telegraph informing her that she had been appointed by Charles C. Moore, president of the Panama–Pacific International Exposition in San Francisco, to organize an international conference of women workers for the promotion of cooperative internationalism.

Before Sewall could begin work on the conference, war in Europe broke out, "temporarily paralyzing the public mind," she noted, and "rendering uncertain" the San Francisco exposition. "While many distinguished advocates of Peace felt that work for its establishment was inevitably suspended by the war—to me the war seemed a proclamation to the women of the world that some action by them which would assert the solidarity of womanhood was imperative," Sewall said.

As soldiers from France and England engaged in bloody battles with their German foes, Sewall set out to make the conference a success, enlisting for her organizing committee such notable women as Jane Addams, Carrie Chapman Catt, Anna Garlin Spencer, and Ida Husted Harper. Members of the committee addressed meetings in Massachusetts, New Hampshire, New York, Maryland, Pennsylvania, Ohio, Indiana, Illinois, Minnesota, Louisiana, Mississippi, Alabama, Oregon, Washington, and California.

The committee also distributed more than two hundred thousand pages of material on the conference to women's clubs, teachers' institutes, parents' associations, patriotic societies, Sunday schools, Chautauqua assemblies, and other gatherings. Sewall sent personal letters to international groups and received in response to her correspondence and published announcements about the conference approximately three thousand responses.

The work paid off when the International Conference of Women Workers to Promote International Peace opened in San Francisco in July 1915. The conference drew approximately five hundred delegates representing the United States and eleven other countries. Numerous speakers promoted the cause of peace, including William Jennings Bryan, former U.S. secretary of state under President Woodrow Wilson.

Delegates also passed a number of resolutions regarding peace. The resolutions included protests against military drill in schools, using public funds to glorify war, and the signing of secret treaties between governments. Women at the conference went on to demand the creation of an international legislative body, international court, and international police; called on nations to agree to ban dangerous weapons; sought full political rights for women nationally and internationally; and urged that neutral nations, which at that time included the United States, create a conference of such countries to attempt to stop the fighting.

Conferences and resolutions were well and good, but Sewall believed in taking a more direct approach to achieve her dreams of peace. In November 1915 she received a telegram that placed her squarely in the middle of a unique attempt to stop the bloody fighting going on in Europe: the Ford Peace Trip.

The telegram was from American automotive manufacturer Henry Ford, who had a plan that he believed would "put a stop to the silly killings going on abroad" and get "the boys out of the trenches by Christmas." Ford asked Sewall to join him and other like-minded people in an expedition to Europe aboard a chartered Danish ocean liner, the *Oscar II*, which sailed from Hoboken, New Jersey, on December 4.

Sewall accepted Ford's offer and became one of sixty peace delegates who, she believed, were not "hair-brained lunatics," as many in the press intimated, but instead a "company of clear-headed but simple-hearted men and women, with no illusions in regard to ourselves but with the faith that any one of us, much more all of us with God, constitute a majority in that council where each next stop along the path of human progress is determined."

Sewall's high hopes for the expedition, however, were put to a severe test by not only the actions of the members of the press on board the ship, but also the behavior of her fellow delegates.

Chapter 6

The Peace Ship

In the early afternoon of December 4, 1915, a crowd estimated at anywhere from three thousand to fifteen thousand people braved the brisk weather at a pier in Hoboken, New Jersey, in order to witness the sailing of the Scandinavian-American ship *Oscar II*. The ship was set for a scheduled ten-day trip across the Atlantic Ocean to Christiania (today Oslo), Norway.

As the ship prepared to leave, the crowd sang and cheered as bands played such rousing songs as "I Didn't Raise My Boy to Be a Soldier" and "Onward, Christian Soldiers." The biggest cheers, however, were reserved for the sponsor of this unusual adventure: famed automaker Henry Ford. The previous summer Ford had declared his willingness to devote his fortune to ending the fighting in Europe between the Allied Powers, led by Great Britain and France, and the Central Powers, dominated by Germany and Austria-Hungary.

Unable to discover any just reasons for the war, Ford believed that some nations "were anxious for peace and would welcome a demonstration for peace." With the encouragement of Rosika Schwimmer, a Hungarian author, lecturer, and peace advocate, Ford had secured passage on the *Oscar II* for about sixty delegates in support of his mission. These delegates would attempt to halt the bloody trench warfare being fought with such deadly weapons as the machine gun and poison gas through the establishment of a neutral commission that would offer

French troops keep a watchful eye out for the enemy from their trenches on the front lines and look over the bodies of those killed in fighting.

LIBRARY OF CONGRESS (2)

negotiation among the nations then at war.

May Wright Sewall was one of the more than one hundred people, including such famous individuals as inventor Thomas Edison, reformer Jane Addams, and former president William Howard Taft to receive invitations from Ford to join him on the voyage.

The first word of the trip came to Sewall in late November when she received a telegram from Ford, followed three days later by a letter in which the automaker spelled out in more detail his reasons for asking her to join him and others on the trip. "From the moment I realized that the world situation demands immediate action, if we do not want the war fire to spread any further," Ford wrote, "I joined those international forces which are working toward ending this unparalleled catastrophe."

Saying it was his "human duty" to work for peace, Ford stated that the world looked to America "to lead in ideals. The greatest mission ever before a nation is ours." The journey outlined by Ford included stops in Norway, Sweden, and Denmark before the delegation's eventual destination, the Hague, the "international city of peace and justice," in the Netherlands. Along the way, the peace expedition hoped to attract ten citizens from each country to join its cause.

Of course, Ford, as a successful businessman, did not handle planning for what came to be known as the Ford Peace Ship. That responsibility fell mainly to Schwimmer and Louis P. Lochner, a writer and former student activist. Although Sewall's work with the National Council of Women and International Council of Women had won her worldwide fame, her invitation to become a delegate more than likely came about through her friendship with Schwimmer, who had been the delegate from Hungary at the IWC's meeting at the Hague in April 1915.

That November, Schwimmer, with help from a *Detroit News* reporter, met with Ford at his estate near Detroit. Lochner also had scheduled a meeting with Ford that day, and the two peace advocates convinced

Ford to support the idea of seeking talks to stop the killing in Europe. Ford agreed to join Schwimmer in New York to work out details for the plan. When Lochner joked about sending the delegates on a special ship chartered for the occasion, Ford, who saw the possible good publicity from such a move, immediately seized on the idea and the Ford Peace Ship was on its way.

Before starting on his peace crusade, Ford, accompanied by Lochner, met with President Woodrow Wilson to try to convince him to appoint an official neutral commission, which Ford was willing to support with his vast fortune. Although noting that he agreed in principle with the idea of negotiating for peace, Wilson skillfully avoided endorsing Ford's proposal.

Ford eventually offered what appeared to be an ultimatum to the president—the next morning Ford would announce to the press that he had secured a ship for a peace delegation. "If you can't act," he told Wilson, "I will." The president refused to officially approve Ford's action, ending the meeting. After leaving Wilson, Ford turned to Lochner and said of the president: "He's a small man."

Even without Wilson's support, Ford seemed confident that the trip would be a success. He told newspaper reporters in New York the next day that he had chartered a ship and planned on trying to "get the boys out of the trenches before Christmas." Accompanying him, he added, would be a group of the "biggest and most influential peace advocates in the country." The ship would also be armed with "the longest gun in the world—the Marconi [radio]," said Ford, which could "let the world know that we are bound for peace."

Press reaction to Ford's announcement was, at best, mixed. Some newspapers gave Ford high marks for his good intentions, but most were doubtful he could accomplish his mission. The *New York Evening Post* boldly predicted that the automaker's plan would "be acclaimed by

LIBRARY OF CONGRESS

Born in 1863, Henry Ford established the Ford Motor Company and revolutionized the automobile industry with the Ford Model T. By 1918 half of all the cars in the United States were Model Ts.

Ford discusses his Peace Ship idea with a group of reporters (above) before meeting with (right) William Jennings Bryan, who for a time served as secretary of state in the Woodrow Wilson administration, at the Hotel Biltmore in New York on December 3, 1915.

LIBRARY OF CONGRESS (2)

thoughtful hundreds of thousands the world over as a bit of American idealism in an hour when the rest of the world has gone mad over war and war-preparedness." Other newspapers were less positive, calling the mission "one of the cruelest jokes of the century."

When the *Oscar II* steamed away from America for Europe it had on board delegates that were not well known by many people. Although numerous politicians and such respected names as Edison had refused to join Ford's peace venture, the group included a respectable number with solid reputations, not only Sewall, but magazine publisher S. S. McClure, Reverend Jenkin Lloyd Jones, and Judge Ben Lindsey. Also on the ship were approximately twenty-five students from Vassar College, Princeton University, Purdue University, the University of Texas, and the University of California at Berkeley; fifty members of the press, including reporters from the United Press, Associated Press, and the International News Service; and twenty-five members of Ford's staff.

In describing her fellow delegates for her friends back home in Indiana, Sewall agreed that no one had an "exalted position; not one bearing the stamp of worldwide recognition." Through their work, however, Sewall said the delegates hoped to accomplish three goals: to secure the public's attention, turning it from war to peace; to stimulate other private efforts and encourage workers to seek peace in every country; and confirm on all those involved their resolution to work for a permanent peace.

Once at sea, the delegates attempted to establish a regular routine. Each day at 11:00 a.m. the students met to learn more about the attempt to bring an end to the fighting in Europe. Each session opened with a talk by one of the delegates on a subject in which they were regarded as an expert.

The delegates listened to similar speakers each afternoon and evening, becoming familiar with one another through such gatherings. Sewall's optimism and efforts on behalf of peace impressed her fellow delegates. One of them, John D. Barry, an essayist, poet, and critic, reflected that in spite of Sewall's age she proved to be one of the "most useful members of the party, keen, and quick of mind, bubbling over with information and observation, humorous, kindly and above all human."

For her talk before the student group, Sewall discussed her work with the International Council of Women, and also touched on the war's effect on that organization. Noting that every ship could withstand a calm sea, Sewall added that the real test of a ship "is what it can do in a storm."

Many international organizations, including the IWC, were "shattered by the catastrophe" of the war, Sewall told the students. But in every country there were women who felt, as she did, that if "we have been weak in our demands for international solidarity before this, the war was a bugle call awakening us to our duty."

Although women as a group were often charged with being subject to their emotions, Sewall said there was no shame in such a fact, as an intellect without emotion would be paralyzed. The key, she told the students, came in controlling emotions in a way that would help lead nations away from war to peace.

Those gathered on the ship were also kept informed of events through an official daily newspaper, the *Argosy*, that printed news, poems, humorous pieces, and more serious fare, including a contribution from Sewall on the woman's movement in America. The newspaper even offered a song for the delegates, to be sung to the tune of the then-popular war song "It's a Long Way to Tipperary."

The song went:

Our peace ship party started with a send off at the pier,
We don't know where we're going—but we're mighty glad we're here,
It's a seasick sort of voyage, over miles of ocean spray
But we put our trust in Henry and with faith and hope we say:

FROM THE COLLECTIONS OF THE HENRY FORD

Ford leans over the railing of the Oscar II *as the ship leaves the dock for its trip across the Atlantic Ocean.*

99

FROM THE COLLECTIONS OF THE HENRY FORD

The Scandinavian-American ship Oscar II *sets off on December 4, 1915, from Hoboken, New Jersey. The ship, bound for Norway, carried on board delegates from the Ford Peace Mission.*

INDIANA HISTORICAL SOCIETY, C7577

Two delegates from the Ford Peace Mission engage in some horseplay aboard the Oscar II *for a news photographer.*

It's a long way to Copenhagen
It's a long way to sail,
It's a long way to Copenhagen,
But we'll get there, never fail.
Good bye dear old Broadway,
Farewell Herald Square
It's a long, long way to Copenhagen,
But peace waits right there.

As for the ship's most famous passenger, Ford, called by Sewall "the Captain of our Peace Mission," became a familiar presence to most of the group. Although he kept away from the delegates' meetings, he did make himself available to the reporters for interviews early in the voyage until a cold forced him to keep mainly to his cabin.

Even when in his cabin, Ford remained, said Sewall, the center of attention of "those of his guests who realize that his own character must inevitably be as unique as the company he has assembled and the mission that he is conducting." To Sewall, the only natural explanation for Ford's "inspired undertaking" was that he was responding to the "call of the Lord."

Ford's goodwill to all on the voyage did have an effect on the ship's passengers, including some reporters. One of the members of the media, Florence Lattimore of *Survey* magazine, later said that another reporter told her that his bosses had told him to write funny articles about the trip, but after seeing Ford's face he could not bring himself to do so. Another newspaperman told Lattimore: "I came to make fun of the whole thing, but my editor is going to have the surprise of his life. I tell you I believe in Henry Ford and I'm going to say so even if I lose my job for it."

Other reporters, however, were unconvinced by their host's goodwill, treating the entire voyage as a big joke. A London reporter even went as far to send a fake story about Ford being held prisoner in his cabin, chained to his bed by his staff. But when the *Oscar II*'s captain, J. W. Hempel, who reviewed all messages sent from the ship, took some of the more insulting stories to Ford, he responded kindly, telling Hempel: "Let them send anything they please. I want the boys to feel perfectly at home while they are with me. They are my guests. I wouldn't for the world censor them."

The free flow of information, both true and false, from the ship caused problems for the expedition. Any arguments among the delegates were turned into sensational newspaper stories. Legend has it that a delegate became so upset about a report from Hoosier Elmer Davis, covering the voyage for the *New York Times*, that he termed the reporter "a snake in the garden of Eden." Davis, who already had helped organize a press club, responded by forming a Snakes in the Garden of Eden Club.

A real problem came, however, when the ship received a radio report on a speech to Congress by Wilson calling for increased military readiness to respond to the war in Europe. There were disagreements among the delegates about Wilson's speech. Some called upon all countries to rid themselves of the weapons of war, and others argued that nations should have the right to defend themselves.

Although the argument ended in a compromise, the disagreement gave reporters an excuse to radio stories back to their newspapers about "war" and a "mutiny" breaking out on the peace ship. In defending the expedition, Lochner asked reporters to show him "any live community in which there is not healthy disagreement over details."

Early in the morning on December 18, the *Oscar II* docked in Christiania, Norway. Physically, Sewall said, Norway gave the delegates a cold welcome, as the weather was reportedly the chilliest in more than a hundred years.

The peace expedition also received a cool reception from the

Norwegian press, which for the most part favored France and England in the war. The delegates were formally welcomed to the Scandinavian country at an afternoon reception sponsored by the Women's International Peace League, followed by a public meeting at the University of Christiania.

With the delegates, including Ford, safely housed in the city's Grand Hotel, Sewall, scheduled to speak at a student meeting, had become convinced that to save herself from freezing to death she must buy a fur-lined cloak, which she accomplished with the help of two friends. She convinced a local merchant to give her the 10 percent discount that all of his regular native customers received, but which never before had been given to a foreigner. Sewall's Norwegian friends, made through her work with the International Council of Women, also sent over a seamstress to "fit my coat and make whatever changes were necessary."

The peace expedition had barely had time to settle into its new setting when it received a bitter blow: Ford had decided to go home. Unable to shake the cold he had caught on the voyage, and encouraged to do so by his staff, Ford had decided to leave in time to catch a ship bound for America.

According to Lochner, who had been "deeply shocked" by Ford's appearance when he visited Ford in his hotel room, the automaker told him: "Guess I had better go home to mother [his wife Clara]. You've got this thing started now and can get along without me." Lochner attempted to convince Ford to stay with the expedition, but failed.

Two days before Christmas, as the delegates prepared to leave Norway by train for Stockholm, Sweden, Ford slipped out of his hotel and took another train to Bergen, Norway. Most of the delegates, including Sewall, believed that Ford had boarded their train, which had been delayed by snow-covered tracks and a frozen engine, to make the frosty journey to Stockholm.

The trip proved to be an uncomfortable one for many of the delegates, as the snow and cold made what would have been a twelve-hour journey into a twenty-two-hour nightmare. Trapped in unheated train cars with no food and no room to sleep, some of the delegates attempted to cheer themselves with singing, including a spirited rendition of "Sweet Adeline" by Reverend Theolopsis Montgomery.

During the long and exhausting train ride, Sewall lost some respect for her fellow delegates. Many of the delegates on the train, she said, could not talk of anything but the irritations that "they were experiencing, the cold, thirst, hunger and general discomfort." She noted that within a few hundred miles of the train there were "thousands upon thousands of soldiers to whom the worst discomfort that this journey brought would be an enviable luxury."

Although Sewall indicated the weather was so cold that it "was beyond language to describe," she managed, as the train sped on to its destination, to comfort herself by watching the countryside as it sped by her window. The scenery the train passed through, she noted, was "so varied, so wild and beautiful that the physical discomfort was quite lost in the joy of it."

As day turned to night, a bright moon lit the landscape, making the glorious forests visible to her. The moonlight also illuminated another feature: people gathered by the train tracks. "Until long past midnight in that awful cold," said Sewall, "people came through drifting snows, facing ice-laden winds, just to see the train that was bearing the Ford Expedition to Stockholm."

Arriving in Stockholm early in the morning on Christmas Eve, the delegates were shocked to discover that Ford had left them. According to Sewall, she and other delegates were eating dinner at the hotel when they received a telegram from Ford on board a ship returning to New York. "His doctor says it is imperative he [Ford] should go at once for a long

May Wright Sewall (first from right, second row) joins fellow delegates from the Ford Peace Mission during a reception in Christiania, Norway.

WISCONSIN HISTORICAL SOCIETY

rest," Sewall reported. "Mr. Ford cables us that if it is possible he shall return to us to meet us at the Hague."

Upon his return to America, Ford told the media he had not deserted the Peace Ship and offered no regrets for sponsoring the expedition. He noted that "the sentiment we have aroused by making the people think will shorten the war." With Ford's departure, the delegates turned for leadership to a committee. Policy matters were handled by Schwimmer and finances were the responsibility of Ford staff member Gaston Plantiff.

The peace expedition spent a week in Stockholm, developing a regular schedule. Each morning at 10:00 a.m. the delegates met to discuss the day's activities. From 11:30 a.m. to 1:00 p.m., the group hosted a reception at the hotel open to the public. The delegates had time to themselves until 4:00 p.m., when the expedition hosted a second public reception.

In helping to welcome visitors to the receptions, Sewall observed that they seemed to fall into four categories: teachers, feminists, social reformers, and students. "I was particularly interested in the university students," she said, "who, although it was their holiday week, called in great numbers. I was amazed by both the intelligence, and by the lively interest in serious subjects of these young people, whom I was mentally comparing with my young countrymen and countrywomen of student age to the distinct disadvantage of the latter."

While in Sweden, Sewall also kept busy by giving speeches, including one to a group of Swedish women. After her talk, one woman told Sewall she had in her possession a portrait of Sewall and a copy of the first suffrage speech the Hoosier had ever given. "She told me that this had been among her treasures for the last 20 years," Sewall said. She also engaged in some diplomacy, meeting with the private secretary for Ira Nelson Morris, the U.S. minister to Norway.

The secretary arranged for a private interview between Sewall and Morris. During the meeting, she told the minister that she was particularly concerned about French misunderstandings about the motives of peace workers in America during the war. Sewall asked if Morris could send through his office a letter from her to the American minister in Paris. Although Sewall found Morris very kind, he could not do what she asked, as he had been instructed by officials in Washington, D.C., to send no letters from his office except for those concerning official government business.

The peace expedition needed its own brand of diplomacy to reach its eventual destination, the Hague. Leaving Sweden for Denmark on December 30, the group discovered that the Danish government had recently passed a law prohibiting foreigners from giving speeches about the war. Working quickly, the delegates were able to discuss their goals at meetings sponsored by private clubs and groups.

In order to reach the group's final stop, the Netherlands, the delegates had to travel, via a sealed train, through German territory, a feat accomplished through the help of the American minister to Denmark. Once in the Netherlands, the group selected delegates for a proposed Neutral Conference for Continuous Mediation, which had its headquarters in Stockholm and worked to negotiate an end to the war.

With this final task completed, the delegates and students could finally return home. On January 15, 1916, the delegates left port aboard the *Rotterdam* for the voyage back to America (the students had left four days earlier on another ship).

The immediate reaction to the Ford Peace Ship once the delegates returned was that the trip was a disaster. "During its two months' run the show has aroused more lively interest, cynical amusement and sheer pity than possibly any other in history," declared Theodore N. Pockman of the *New York Tribune*, who had traveled with the group.

What the media failed to see, argued peace advocates, was that the work of the Neutral Conference for Continuous Mediation continued for another year after the peace ship delegates returned home. In his history of the American peace movement, historian Merle Curti points out that the conference fulfilled a useful purpose, as it brought together the "scattered efforts of publicists and idealists in neutral countries engaged in an effort to formulate and popularize terms for a just and lasting peace."

For Sewall, the "spectacular pilgrimage" had been a success, as it had "concentrated the thought of the distracted world upon this hope with a force that assures its achievement." She felt proud of the work done by her and her fellow delegates. "To have advanced its [peace's] arrival by one hour," Sewall said, "is adequate compensation for the cost in money, time and sacrifices of the Expedition if multiplied a thousandfold."

Sewall's view was shared in part by one of the reporters aboard the *Oscar II*, Elmer Davis. Although he considered the trip a "crazy enterprise," Davis, looking back on the voyage in an essay published in 1939 as Europe seemed on the brink of another war, said that any effort, "however visionary and inadequate, to stop a war that was wrecking Europe, appears in retrospect a little less crazy than most of the other purposes that were prevalent in Europe in 1916."

Upon her return to America, Sewall gave numerous lectures attempting to give audiences the true story of the expedition, speaking to church groups, women's clubs, schools, and teacher conventions. As the United States inched closer to involvement in World War I, prompted in part by Germany's resumption of unrestricted submarine warfare and the interception of a telegram from German foreign minister Arthur Zimmermann proposing a German-Mexican alliance against the United States, Sewall continued to work for peace.

In a letter to her friends in Indiana from New York, published after President Wilson had asked Congress for a declaration of war on April 2, 1917, Sewall expressed great concern about the growing war frenzy on the East Coast and urged her friends back in the Midwest to guard against such feelings. In addition to New York newspapers clamoring for war, Sewall indicated that meetings were being held daily "whose evident purpose is to bring the public mind to the point of declaring an Anglo-American alliance" against Germany.

Government and military officials were forcing loyalty oaths on citizens, and women were even organizing into military companies to defend the city against attack. "Where is the psychologist who will not only diagnose the malady that has prostrated the reason, the common sense and the judgment of this community," she asked, "but worse still has paralyzed humane sentiment and Christian principle and obscured that American 'sense of humor' upon which we as a people always rely to preserve our poise under whatever emergency?" She ended her letter: "Hoping that these conditions do not exist in the middle West, I am first, a human; second, a very loyal American; third and always, a loving Hoosier."

Sewall's plea for reason to her former friends and neighbors failed to change public opinion in Indianapolis. With the declaration of war, all things German were under suspicion. A patriotic fever gripped Indianapolis and the rest of the state. Teachers were required to take oaths of allegiance in some communities; those who refused were in real danger of losing their jobs for their "disloyalty." School boards banned the teaching of the German language in public and private schools, and German landmarks throughout the state quickly underwent name changes. For example, the Das Deutsche Haus in Indianapolis became the Athenaeum and Bismark Street became Pershing Street. Those who refused to buy bonds in Liberty Loan campaigns on behalf of the war effort were even pulled from their homes at night by angry mobs and had their homes painted yellow.

Those who did not share in the enthusiasm at America's joining the

LIBRARY OF CONGRESS

A poster encourages Hoosiers to support the war effort during World War I.

fighting had to endure their friends' disapproval even after the war ended in 1918 with an Allied victory. In Sewall's case, her peace activities seemed to make her former neighbors in Indianapolis forget all the good work she had done for the community.

Sewall's work for peace, however, gave way within the next few years to another enterprise—one that would cause as much controversy as the Ford Peace Ship. Unknown to the general public, Sewall had, since 1897, been deeply involved in spiritualism, communicating with her dead husband Theodore and other deceased relatives. In relating her shocking discovery to the public, Sewall had the assistance of an old Indianapolis friend: best-selling author Booth Tarkington.

Chapter 7

The Book

In 1918 Booth Tarkington, enjoying the summer at his home in Kennebunkport, Maine, received in the mail an invitation from an old friend from Indianapolis to meet and discuss a manuscript the friend had written. In the letter the friend, May Wright Sewall, did not discuss what her writing was about. Knowing of her previous work in Indiana, Tarkington assumed that the book would be "something educational."

When he finally received the manuscript, Tarkington was amazed to discover "that for more than twenty years this academic-liberal of a thousand human activities . . . had been really living not with the living, so to put it." Writing her with his review of the work, Tarkington told Sewall he read the manuscript "very carefully and with an ever increasing interest."

Sewall's manuscript, eventually published by the Bobbs-Merrill Company of Indianapolis just two months before her death in July 1920, detailed her numerous experiences with the strange world of spiritualism—the belief that those who live can communicate with the dead.

Sewall's contact with the dead, which included not only numerous conversations with her husband Theodore but also talks with a priest who had lived in the Middle Ages and a famous musician, shocked many who knew her as a no-nonsense woman. Anton Scherrer, a columnist for the *Indianapolis Times*, said that nothing "rocked the foundations of Indianapolis quite as much" as the appearance of Sewall's book, because nobody in her old hometown knew about her contacts with the spirit world.

Only a dozen or so people knew about this part of Sewall's life. During her communications with her departed husband, he had warned her, Sewall told a reporter from the *Indianapolis Star*, not to tell about them "to the world until she had them in such form the world could understand them." Also, those to whom she related her experiences often said that they were just figments of Sewall's imagination.

Perhaps realizing that she might be made fun of by many people for these unusual experiences, Sewall decided to tell her spiritualist story only when illness had taken her once and for all out of public affairs. Free from involvement in the reform work she had been active in for most of her life, Sewall had time to gather from the hundreds of her record books the spiritualist events she told about in her book, titled *Neither Dead nor Sleeping*.

The question of whether it was possible to communicate with the spirit world had been a hot topic of debate in American society since 1848 when the Fox sisters—Katherine, age eleven, and Margaretta, age thirteen—had reported strange noises in their family's home in Hydesville, New York. The children's parents, John and Margaret Fox, soon spread word of the strange happenings to neighbors, who came to the home and themselves heard the odd noises.

Years later both sisters confessed that they, and not ghosts, were the cause of the strange rappings. The Fox sisters' confessions came too late, however, to stop a nationwide spiritualist movement that promised to make "heaven utterly democratic and accessible to all." In 1868 the American Association of Spiritualists had been organized, and by 1871 spiritualist societies had been formed in twenty-two states.

In 1862 the first organization of Indiana spiritualists was created with Doctor Samuel Maxwell of Richmond as president. Two years earlier,

NORTH WIND PICTURE ARCHIVES

Drawing of the spiritual materialization of Annie Morgan, said to have been dead for two hundred years, revealing herself to mediums in Philadelphia in the 1870s.

Robert Dale Owen, son of the founder of New Harmony, Robert Owen, and a respected reformer, diplomat, and politician, published *Footfalls on the Boundary of Another World*. The book quickly sold out of its first printing of two thousand copies. In 1872 Owen followed up his previous success by writing another best-selling spiritualist book.

By 1888 the Indiana Association of Spiritualists decided to build a campground for its meetings and selected Chesterfield as the location. The thirty-four-acre site hosted its first meeting in 1892 and grew to become the second largest spiritualist camp in the country (only Lily Dale in New York was larger) and averaged crowds of twenty thousand people at its annual six-week sessions during the summer.

In spite of the enthusiastic reception spiritualism received by some people, to many it became a subject for laughter. For suffragists, however, spiritualists were treated as friends who shared their belief in equal rights for all and who invited them to speak at their meetings.

It was at a spiritualist camp meeting in Lily Dale, New York, that Sewall began her adventures with the world beyond the grave. According to Sewall, her husband, Theodore, had promised her before his death that if possible he would attempt to communicate with her. After Theodore died, Sewall tried to forget her grief by burying herself in her work, including her duties at the Girls' Classical School. She succeeded so well that she put her husband's promise completely out of her mind.

When some Indianapolis friends advised her to visit a local medium in order to communicate once again with Theodore, the proposal shocked her. "It seemed to me grossly to violate both reason and delicacy," she said. Instead of taking them up on their offer, Sewall continued to give her time to her school and work with both the National and International Council of Women.

While giving a lecture in Nova Scotia, Canada, in June 1897, Sewall received an invitation to give a talk at a "Woman's Day" program at what she later learned was a spiritualist camp in Lily Dale, New York. "I had held myself so aloof from all means of information about spiritualism," she said, "that I did not know there were such camps."

Sewall arrived at Lily Dale's assembly grounds early in the evening on August 9, 1897, and was greeted by the chairman of the press committee for the National American Woman Suffrage Association, who asked her if she wished to tour the facility and be introduced to some of the famous mediums gathered there for the meeting. "I told her," said Sewall, "that I did not wish to meet any 'medium' however 'famous'; that to me the word was offensive, being synonymous in my opinion, with the words, deceiver, pretender, charlatan and ignoramus."

A series of unexpected delays caused Sewall to stay over at Lily Dale for a time. Giving in to a "compelling impulse which I scarcely realized until I acted upon it," she participated in a sitting with a famous independent slate writer, a medium who used blank slates to pass messages on to the living from spirits.

During her meeting with the slate writer, Sewall claimed that the blank slates never left her side, but when she returned with them to her hotel she discovered that they were covered with "clear and legible writing" and contained "perfectly coherent, intelligent and characteristic replies to questions which I had written upon bits of paper that had not passed out of my hands."

Out of this experience, Sewall said she had obtained "actual knowledge, if not of immortality, at least of a survival of death—I had learned that the last enemy is destroyed, in that he can destroy neither being nor identity, nor continuity of relationship." Through later meetings with a host of different mediums, Sewall communicated with a number of her deceased loved ones, including her husband, father, mother, half-sister, great-grandfather, niece, and two sisters-in-law.

Through the years, as she became more skilled in getting in touch with the spirit world, Sewall communicated with Theodore through a method called automatic writing. Equipped with only a tablet and pencil, Sewall would sit in her library and her husband's spirit would guide her hand to produce written answers to her questions about life after death.

In addition to teaching her about the spirit world, Theodore introduced Sewall to distinct people, including Anton Rubinstein, a famous pianist, and Père Condé, a medieval priest and physician from France. Although Sewall never considered herself musical, Theodore insisted that she buy a piano on which to be instructed by Rubinstein. Her husband told her that the deepest element in her character was a love of harmony, which gave Sewall her success as an organizer.

Sewall's communications with the spirit world became known to the living through the efforts of an Indiana writer who had had his own experience with unexplained happenings—Tarkington. When he was fourteen years old and living in Indianapolis, Tarkington discovered that his sister, Hauté, had psychic powers. The Tarkington family hosted séances at its home that drew such distinguished visitors as James Whitcomb Riley.

Although Hauté's powers faded away after her marriage, her devoted brother remained convinced that his sister had true psychic ability. Throughout his life, noted Tarkington biographer James Woodress, the writer "was tolerant of other persons' alleged supersensory experience." When Sewall approached him for assistance in finding a publisher for her spiritualist manuscript, Tarkington proved eager to help.

By the fall of 1918 Tarkington had a stenographer make a copy of Sewall's manuscript to present to possible publishers. He wrote Sewall that he needed to find a firm willing not only to print the book, but also to promote it to a wide audience. "I assure you that I will do everything within my power not only to get it printed," he said, "but to get it 'pushed'!"

Tarkington repeated his belief that Sewall's manuscript stood as

INDIANA HISTORICAL SOCIETY, C5076

INDIANA HISTORICAL SOCIETY

A young Booth Tarkington stands alongside his beloved sister, Hauté, who displayed psychic powers as a young woman. She later lost those powers after becoming married.

a "unique document with the air of a classic in human experience." By March 1919 Tarkington had decided to place the manuscript with the Bobbs-Merrill Company, which could trace its roots in Indianapolis back to the 1850s and was the publisher for such Hoosier literary stars as Riley, George Ade, Meredith Nicholson, and Maurice Thompson. Tarkington passed along Sewall's manuscript to Bobbs-Merrill with the understanding that he would write an introduction for the book. He did warn Sewall that a decision on whether or not to publish her work could take some time.

Tarkington's warning proved to be correct. During the spring and summer, he exchanged a series of letters with Sewall discussing the lack of a decision from Bobbs-Merrill on the book. Although the firm's literary adviser and trade editor Hewitt H. Howland had told Tarkington he was in favor of accepting the book, and Tarkington wrote Sewall that he was tempted to push the firm about the manuscript, he feared doing so because a "very little push upon a publisher sometimes turns him aside from the right path."

A final decision on the manuscript depended upon the opinion of William C. Bobbs, the company's president, "and *that* must take its own time not ours!" said Tarkington. By the end of July, Tarkington's patience had been tried enough for him to suggest to Sewall that she write a note to Howland "and hint that you can wait no longer." If Bobbs-Merrill did decide against publishing her work, Tarkington told Sewall that he had already opened discussions with a literary adviser for another publisher, and he had expressed "much interest" in her manuscript.

Sometime in August Bobbs-Merrill finally agreed to publish Sewall's book. One of the reasons for the firm's acceptance might have been its eagerness to add Tarkington to its list of authors. According to one account, David Laurance Chambers, a Bobbs-Merrill editor and later the company's president, was Tarkington's close friend and "never concealed his hope that the author might some day publish through Bobbs-Merrill."

During her exchange of letters with Tarkington about her manuscript, the seventy-five-year-old Sewall, who had been in ill health, had been making plans to leave the East Coast and return to live in Indianapolis. She had even written her old suffragist friend, Grace Julian Clarke, to seek advice on possible places for her to stay. Clarke wrote back expressing her delight at Sewall's decision to live again in Indianapolis, but reported that the three places she had in mind as possible homes for Sewall were unavailable.

Despite Clarke's bad news, Sewall remained determined to return to Indianapolis, the scene of many of the triumphs and tragedies in her life. Writing from the Aloha Rest home in Winthrop Highlands, Massachusetts, Sewall thanked Howland, the editor for her book, for accepting her manuscript. She said that it pleased her to have the book published in the city where many of the experiences took place and where there were many witnesses to the "external regimen and to the changes in myself" recorded in the book.

Although she gave permission to Howland to shorten the second part of the book, she did ask him one favor. Sewall said she was quite anxious to have the book come out as soon as possible because numerous publishing firms were releasing books on spiritualism in order to take advantage of the huge surge in interest in the subject from families who had lost their husbands, sons, fathers, and brothers during World War I. "The war has terribly increased the number of bereaved and bleeding hearts and often the skepticism of the intellect can be broken down only through the agony of a yearning heart," Sewall said. "I, who *have* suffered, want to help those who do suffer."

In early October 1919 Sewall finally returned to Indianapolis, living at a house at 1732 North Illinois Street. Although so ill with heart disease that she had trouble breathing and had to be propped up in bed by

INDIANA HISTORICAL SOCIETY, BASS PHOTO COMPANY COLLECTION

Author Booth Tarkington, two-time winner of the Pulitzer Prize for literature, proved to be a valuable ally for May Wright Sewall and her spiritualist manuscript.

pillows, Sewall managed to make corrections on galley proofs of her book.

In spite of her serious illness, there were times when the old confident Sewall again appeared. "I think I never did a better piece of proof reading—and I am perfectly delighted with the book," she told Howland in December. "I *know* it will have an ultimate great success."

Sewall's confidence may have been inspired by the bond she established with her editor. She apologized to Howland for delaying the work on her book because of her illness, but promised to keep herself well enough to correct proof as fast as it arrived. Sewall was lucky because she would be working with an editor known for selecting and publishing manuscripts that had the greatest potential as best sellers for the firm.

An Indianapolis native, Howland had an impressive background; his father served as a judge and his brother, Louis, worked as an editor for the *Indianapolis News*. His father's death dashed Hewitt Howland's hopes for a college education, so at age fifteen he took a job in the Yohn Book Shop on Washington Street. After traveling in Great Britain for a time, Howland returned to Indianapolis and worked as a railway clerk and broker. In 1898 Howland started working for Bobbs-Merrill as a part-time manuscript reader, becoming an editor just two years later.

Howland used his charm and skill as an editor to create a good relationship with Sewall. He offered few major changes to her manuscript, even deciding against some deletions in part two that he had suggested earlier. Howland did, however, object to some aspects of Sewall's preface, including a part where she expressed the hope that men and women trained in scientific investigation would take up where she left off. "This will lead the dear average reader to feel that the book is not intended for him and I am sure you want him to read it," Howland told Sewall.

Forced out of public affairs by poor health and her dedication to seeing her book published, Sewall nevertheless caught the attention of the local media. Learning of her return to her hometown, the *Indianapolis*

INDIANA PICTURE COLLECTION, MANUSCRIPT SECTION, INDIANA STATE LIBRARY

Bobbs-Merrill Company editor Hewitt Howland (standing, right) is shown with two of his leading writers, Meredith Nicholson (standing, left) and James Whitcomb Riley.

News took the opportunity to question her about a variety of subjects, including world affairs and woman's suffrage.

Turning to one of her favorite subjects, the quest for peace, Sewall told the *News* that such a goal would be brought about by "spiritual reformation, by the movement of the soul, not by the use of ammunition." Although the Nineteenth Amendment to the U.S. Constitution, which finally gave women the right to vote in all elections, still needed to be ratified by the required number of states in order to become the law of the land, Sewall said she had considered the issue settled since 1889.

Sewall did tell the reporter that she was anxious to see what women would do once they finally could vote in large numbers. "I have no reason to believe," she said, "that they will use it differently from the way in which men make use of it. Why should they? We are all very much alike, born of the same parents."

As winter turned into spring and her book remained unpublished, Sewall began to be apprehensive about the future. "I beg you to believe," she said in a dictated letter to Howland, "that I am distressed at feeling the need of troubling you, but I have been very ill for several weeks with the prospect of continuing so, or worse; and I am beginning to be very anxious about the possibility of holding out until my book is out."

Sewall's friends were also worried about her health. Ida Husted Harper confided to Clarke that she had been "feeling very uneasy about her [Sewall], as she has not written me for weeks and did not even acknowledge my Christmas message, which is most unusual for her." By the time Howland could present Sewall with a complimentary copy of her book, she had been moved from her Illinois Street residence to a room at Saint Vincent Hospital.

Howland predicted that Sewall's book was "destined to make a profound impression, and to do more to convince the unbelieving than any human document yet given to the world." To help sales of *Neither*

Dead nor Sleeping, Bobbs-Merrill worked hard to promote the book with booksellers and newspapers.

Calling the work "The Wonder Book of the Ages," and labeling its author "one of the best known among the pioneer progressive women of the country," the firm issued a first printing of three thousand copies and promoted it to book dealers as "a sure-fire seller from the start. It's the kind the dealer will take home and read and reread himself!" The Indianapolis company had Sewall autograph copies of the book, which sold for $3 per copy, to be sent to influential literary editors representing such publications as the *Literary Digest*, *Publishers Weekly*, and *Booklist*, as well as newspapers in New York, Chicago, Los Angeles, and San Francisco.

These promotional efforts by Bobbs-Merrill paid off. Howland reported to Sewall that ten to twelve newspapers had printed a full-page story on the book and as of early June one-third of the first printing of three thousand had been sold. He predicted a bright outlook for the book and indicated that the firm's confidence and interest remained unabated.

Sewall showed considerable interest in her book's promotion, even subscribing to a newspaper clipping service to check on reviews. She also found the strength to discuss her spiritualist experiences with a reporter, Elizabeth Morgan, with the *Indianapolis Star*. The resulting full-page article in the *Star*'s Sunday magazine featured some bold predictions from Sewall about spiritualism's future, including its eventual teaching as a subject in high schools and universities.

Morgan, who interviewed Sewall a few weeks before *Neither Dead nor Sleeping*'s publication, said the former teacher seemed eager that those who read her book might profit from her experiences and gain from it "the sure comfort of knowing the simplicity and naturalness of the life into which they passed from the life of earth."

To ease the reader into the story of her astonishing experiences,

125

Portrait of Sewall used by the Bobbs-Merrill Company for
promotion of her spiritualist book Neither Dead nor Sleeping.

LILLY LIBRARY, INDIANA UNIVERSITY

Tarkington had contributed an introduction for *Neither Dead nor Sleeping*. In considering whether or not Sewall's spiritualist beliefs might be true, Tarkington had three possible explanations for her story: Sewall had merely imagined her talks with those who had died, the communications were part of her subconscious mind ("the part of our minds that constructs our dreams"), or the "communications are, as Mrs. Sewall believes them to be, from people we speak of as dead; but really they live."

Tarkington believed that the truth rested somewhere between the second and third explanations. He said that either Sewall's subconscious had been "up to a dumbfounding prodigy of dream-building, or else Mrs. Sewall has been in communication with living people whom we have thought of as dead."

Many reviewers echoed Tarkington's kind treatment of Sewall's work. Writing for the *Chicago Tribune*, Elia W. Peattie claimed that the book had been written in "good faith." The author had found, Peattie added, an "escape from illness and sorrow, and there remains but to extend to her sincere and deeply felt congratulations." Reviewing several books on psychic experiences for the *New York Evening Post*, J. Keith Torbert wrote that both for those who believe and for those who make fun of spiritualism, Sewall's book "has essentials to reveal." *Neither Dead nor Sleeping* had, Torbert added, something that raised it above the ordinary. "This is the very human touch to the writing," he wrote. "The strong, admirable character of Mrs. Sewall appears on every page." The book even received a positive notice in the *New York Times Book Review*. In examining eleven books that discussed the question of what happens after a person dies, the review highlighted Sewall's as "one of the most striking—amazing is hardly too strong a word."

These strong words of praise came at a time when Sewall lay gravely ill at Saint Vincent Hospital in Indianapolis. Former students of the Girls'

Classical School were at her bedside to nurse their former teacher and mentor. Sewall's health continued to fail at a time when American women were finally about to achieve a goal they had been working toward since the days of the pioneering Seneca Falls meeting in 1848.

Epilogue

During the month of August 1920, reporters from major American newspapers focused their attention on the actions of a special session of the Tennessee legislature in Nashville. Reporters were everywhere in Nashville suffering from the hot and muggy weather so they could describe the final act of a struggle that had been going on for many years—gaining for women the right to vote.

Amending the U.S. Constitution to achieve suffrage for women proved to be a difficult task. Not only did any amendment have to be passed by two-thirds of the members of the U.S. House of Representatives and Senate, but also by three-quarters of the states.

The first step began early in 1919 when Congress passed the Nineteenth Amendment to the Constitution. "This was the day toward which women had been struggling for more than half a century!" exclaimed one suffragist. "We were in the dawn of woman's political power in America."

The Nineteenth Amendment declared that the "right of citizens of the United States to vote shall not be denied or abridged by the United States or by any State on account of sex." But in order to become law, the amendment also had to be approved (ratified) by thirty-six states or it would fail. When the amendment reached Tennessee, thirty-five states had already approved the measure.

Tensions were high in Nashville. Legislators who supported a woman's right to vote wore yellow roses, those who opposed suffrage wore red roses. Newspapers began to call the fight over ratification "The War of the Roses." Before the session opened, Tennessee governor Albert H. Roberts noted that "millions of women are looking to this Legislature to give them a voice and share in shaping the destiny of the Republic." On August 13, 1920, after just three hours of debate, the Tennessee Senate voted for ratification and sent the resolution on to the House of Representatives.

The battle over ratification grew tenser when the House of Representatives met on August 18. A motion to delay action on, or table, the resolution drew a tie vote of forty-eight to forty-eight. Harry Burn, a Republican who at age twenty-four was the legislature's youngest member, had been viewed as an opponent of woman's suffrage. His feelings on the issue had changed, however, thanks to a message from one of his constituents—his mother, Febb Emsinger Burn.

In her letter, Febb Burn had written: "Dear Son: Hurrah, and vote for suffrage! Don't keep them in doubt. I noticed some of the speeches against. They were bitter. I have been watching to see how you stood, but have not noticed anything yet. Don't forget to be a good boy and help

Harry T. Burn proved to be the key vote in Tennessee's ratification of the Nineteenth Amendment.

FROM THE HARRY T. BURN PAPERS, McCLUNG HISTORICAL COLLECTION

Mrs. [Carrie Chapman] Catt put the 'rat' in ratification."

When House members voted on whether or not to approve the resolution, Burn switched sides and supported ratification. When the roll call ended, the resolution had passed by a fifty to forty-six vote. On August 24, 1920, Governor Roberts signed the bill. Two days later, U.S. Secretary of State Bainbridge Colby signed a proclamation officially making the Nineteenth Amendment part of the Constitution.

Years later, Burn noted that although his mother was a college-educated woman, she could not vote, while there were males who could not read or write yet still had the right to vote. "On that roll call, confronted with the fact that I was going to go on record for time and eternity on the merits of the question," said Burn, "I had to vote for ratification."

The glorious news for American women came too late for one pioneer who had worked her whole life to achieve the right to cast a vote alongside men. At 11:15 p.m. on July 22, 1920, May Wright

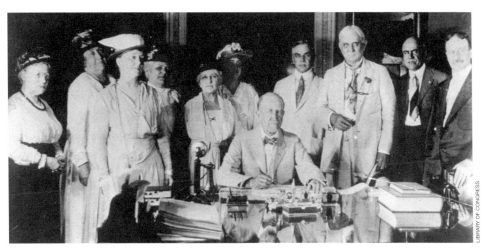

LIBRARY OF CONGRESS

Posing with suffrage leaders and members of Congress, Speaker of the House of Representatives Frederick H. Gillette (center), a Republican from Massachusetts, signs a resolution sending the Nineteenth Amendment off for ratification by the states.

No. 27,880. Entered as second-class matter
post office Washington, D. C.

SUFFRAGE PROCLAIMED BY COLBY, WHO SIGNS AT HOME EARLY IN DAY

50 = Year Struggle Ends in Victory for Women

NO CEREMONY IN FINAL ACTION

Secretary Felicitates Leaders; Hails New Era.

Ratification of the nineteenth amendment to the Constitution of the United States, granting suffrage to women, was proclaimed officially today by Secretary Colby of the State Department.

The proclamation was signed by Secretary Colby at 8 o'clock this morning at his home, when the certi-

PROCLAMATION ENFRANCHISES WOMEN OF U. S.

Bainbridge Colby, Secretary of State of the United States of America.

To all to whom these presents shall come, greeting:

Know ye, that the Congress of the United States at the first session, Sixty-sixth Congress, begun at Washington on the nineteenth day of May, in the year one thousand nine hundred and nineteen, passed a resolution as follows, to wit:

Joint resolution, proposing an amendment to the Constitution extending the right of suffrage to women.

Resolved by the Senate and House of Representatives of the United States of America in Congress assembled (two-thirds of each House concurring therein), that the following article is proposed as an amendment to the Constitution, which shall be valid to all intents and purposes as part of the Constitution when ratified by the legislatures of three-fourths of the several states.

LIBRARY OF CONGRESS

Headline from the May 19, 1919, issue of the Washington Star *announcing that U.S. Secretary of State Bainbridge Colby had signed the necessary document that finally gave all American women the right to vote.*

Sewall, at the age of seventy-six, died while a patient at Saint Vincent Hospital in Indianapolis. The *Indianapolis Star* reported that Sewall's age, in connection "with a gradual physical decline . . . in the last three months convinced her physicians some time ago that her recovery was impossible."

After funeral services at All Souls Unitarian Church, Sewall was buried alongside her beloved husband, Theodore, at Crown Hill Cemetery. With Sewall's death, the *Indianapolis News* said on its editorial page, the world lost a citizen. Although she had lived, worked, and died in Indianapolis, her "activities were such that she was known not only in this country but throughout Europe as well." Throughout her life, the *News* added, "Mrs. Sewall possessed the faculty of transmitting her boundless enthusiasm and her original ideas to the world around her. One could not slumber in her presence for her vitality was contagious."

In the years following Sewall's death attempts were made in Indianapolis to celebrate her notable accomplishments. At the February 1921 meeting in Indianapolis of the State Collegiate Alumnae, James Woodburn, an Indiana University history professor and close friend of both Sewalls for many years, presented a talk outlining Sewall's career. In addition, Sewall's friends and admirers discussed plans to honor her memory by naming a bookshelf in her honor at the local library and dedicating a pair of elaborate bronze lamps and standards in her name at the entrance to the John Herron Art Institute.

On a rainy Sunday afternoon in May 1923, two bronze memorial candelabra were dedicated in Sewall's memory at the Herron Art Institute (later the candelabras stood guard over the Forty-Second Street entrance to the Indianapolis Museum of Art). At the dedication ceremony, held indoors at the institute due to the bad weather, Woodburn praised Sewall for giving "her soul in self-surrender to the service of humanity."

Because of her belief in spiritualism, Sewall's reputation has suffered over the years. Nothing, however, can take away from what she accomplished during her life. Unafraid of what critics and doubters might say, Sewall gave her heart and soul for causes still of vital importance—education, women's rights, and world peace. Her legacy continues in the ongoing work of the International Council of Women and with a new generation of women still struggling to be heard by those in power.

The Indianapolis Woman's Club, the Contemporary Club, and the Propylaeum—groups Sewall had a major role in creating—carry on her efforts to improve life for those in Indianapolis. Located today at 1410 North Delaware Street, the Propylaeum proudly displays in its front hall a framed portrait of Sewall painted by noted Indiana artist T. C. Steele and the trowel Sewall used when she broke ground for the original Propylaeum in 1890. To also honor its founder, the Propylaeum Historic

DAVID TURK, INDIANA HISTORICAL SOCIETY

Located at 1410 North Delaware Street in Indianapolis, the Propylaeum continues to serve the central Indiana community as a gateway to culture.

Foundation in 2005 created the May Wright Sewall Leadership Award to help recognize Indianapolis women for their distinguished community service.

Sewall, who throughout her life loved books, and the countless lives she touched during her life can be viewed online through a digital collection at the Indianapolis–Marion County Public Library's Web site at http://www.imcpl.org/resources/digitallibrary/maywrightsewall.html. The collection includes approximately five hundred letters written to Sewall between 1879 and 1919, as well as three guest books with signatures and comments from approximately two hundred people who stayed at Sewall's home.

Sewall had much to be thankful for during her long years of service to her hometown, her state, her country, and the rest of the world. She told her friend Grace Julian Clarke that she was thankful for being born in a family of "liberal tendencies, liberals in politics and religion"; being equipped with a good mind and body that enabled her to live a long and fruitful life; having a husband (Theodore Sewall) "whose tastes and ideals were in entire sympathy with her own"; and having the ability to love her friends.

Although during her last days Sewall realized, Clarke related, that she might be "a member of the Has Been family," it comforted her to know that "she was a HAS BEEN, a plus, not a minus."

Sewall had one goal during her life: to make herself useful to the entire world—something she accomplished. "What she wrought," Clarke said of Sewall, "will endure, and generations yet unborn will find life a fuller and richer experience because she joined in the effort to make it so instead of . . . accepting conditions as they were."

Appendix 1

On June 30, 1888, Susan B. Anthony, National Woman Suffrage Association vice-president-at-large, and May Wright Sewall, NWSA executive committee chairman, issued an open letter to Republican presidential candidate Benjamin Harrison asking him to consider the following facts:

The first plank in the platform adopted by the Republican convention recently held in Chicago, entitled "The Purity of the Ballot," reaffirms the unswerving devotion of the Republican party to the personal rights and liberties of citizens in all the States and Territories of the Union, and especially to "the supreme and sovereign right of every lawful citizen, rich or poor, native or foreign, white or black, to cast one free ballot in public elections and to have that ballot duly counted." And again the platform says: "We hold the free and honest popular ballot, and the just and equal representation of all the people, to be the foundation of our republican government."

These declarations place the Republican party in its original attitude as the defender of the personal freedom and political liberties of all citizens of the United States. These sentiments, even the phraseology in which they are here expressed, may be found in every series of resolutions adopted by the National Woman Suffrage Association since its organization.

The advocates of woman suffrage would have been glad to see the phrase "male or female" inserted after the phrase "white or black" in the resolution above quoted, because this would be a fitting conclusion to the enumeration by antithesis of the classes into which citizens are divided. However, no enumeration of classes was necessary to explain or to enforce the declaration of the party's devotion to "the supreme and sovereign right of every lawful citizen to cast one free ballot in public elections and to have that ballot duly counted." It is the unimpeded exercise of this "supreme and sovereign right of every lawful citizen" which the women we represent demand.

That women are "lawful citizens" is undeniable, since the law recognizes them as such through the visits of the assessor and tax-gatherer; since it recognizes them as such in the police stations, the jails, the courts and the prisons. Only at the ballot-box is the lawful citizenship of women challenged! Only at the ballot-box, which is declared to be the sole safe-guard of the citizen's liberty—only there is the liberty of the female citizen denied.

But reverting to the first resolution in the Republican platform, so satisfactory in its sentiments, we beg to suggest that its value will depend solely upon its interpretation, and that its authoritative interpretation must be given by the leaders of the Republican party. Therefore to you, the chosen head of the party, we address ourselves, asking that your letter of acceptance to the nomination to the presidency of the United States be so framed as to indicate clearly your recognition of the fact that the Republican party has pledged itself to protect *every citizen* in the free exercise of "the supreme and sovereign right" to vote at public elections.

It appears to us that the application of Republican principles which we seek must be in harmony with your own inherited tendencies. One familiar with the history of the English-speaking people, during the last two and a half centuries, with their struggles for conscience, and freedom's sake, must deem it a matter of course that by this time the sense of individual responsibility has become strong even in the hearts of women; and the descendant of one who in the name of individual liberty stood with Cromwell against the "divine right of kings" and the tyranny consequent upon that obnoxious doctrine, can not be surprised to find himself appealed to by his country-women, in that same sacred name, to stand with the most enlightened portion of his party—with such men as Morton, Sumner and Lincoln—against the divine right of sex and the political tyranny involved in this doctrine, which in a republic presents such an anomaly.

Appendix 2

To recruit followers for her idea of an International Council of Women, Sewall traveled to Europe to address an International Congress of Women, which met in Paris in July 1889. This was her first opportunity to outline her idea for a worldwide woman's organization to a foreign audience. The following are some of her remarks at the Paris congress:

The organization which I have the honor to represent in this distinguished congress has a most significant title. It is called The National Council of Women of the United States. The origin of this organization is as significant as its name.

The National Council of Women of the United States is one of the immediate products of an International Council of Women, convened at Washington, the capital of our country, in March 1888.

The International council held in Washington was convened under the auspices of the National Woman Suffrage Association of the U.S., but it included representatives of all degrees of conservatism as well as of all degrees of radicalism; that was incomparably the most truly representative gathering of women ever convened in our country. The subjects which we considered were naturally as numerous and as various as were the organizations represented in it. Delegates from fifty-eight national organizations of women in our own country and from various organizations of women in England, Scotland, France, Norway, Denmark,

Finland, India and Canada, discussed under numerous sub-titles the general subjects of philanthropy, charities, temperance, moral reform and political rights, or such aspect of those subjects as particularly interest and affect women.

That council illustrated on a great scale, what had before a thousand times been proved in a small way,—viz., that it is good for people independently holding different views and working along entirely different directions, to meet now and then on the broad lines of general agreement and human sympathy.

The conviction that such occasional meetings would benefit all who should participate in them grew from day to day through the fifteen sessions of the council in the minds of its participants, as it had grown in the mind of the chairman of its Organizing committee during the months of preparation. Out of that conviction arose the permanent National Council of Women of the United States, and also the initiatory steps toward forming a permanent International council.

The constitution of the National council, adopted at Washington, and the circular letter issued subsequently by its general officers . . . show that the object of the council is to bring all national organizations of women into a federation, and to provide for regular triennial meetings of such federation. In these meetings every cause or object represented by the National organizations which have joined the federation will be discussed by its advocates, and its progress will be officially reported. It will be seen that the National council itself, as such, does not espouse any one cause, advocate any *one* reform, or, indeed, give preference to any one above the others. All of the organizations confederated in it meet in it as equals, with equal representation on its official staff and on its executive board, whatever their respective numerical strength may be. Whether the significance of this will be understood by those unfamiliar with the conditions of American life I am uncertain, and, therefore, I shall undertake to explain one aspect of American social life which has so often excited the curiosity of travelers in our country.

De Tocqueville speaks with astonishment at the ease with which public meetings are convened in the United States, and of the tendency of American men to organize into bodies for the accomplishment of any desired purpose—for instance, as the building of a church, opening a school, mending a road, draining a swamp, approving or condemning an official.

The same "tendency to hold meetings and to organize," which De Tocqueville notices as characteristic of American men, has also developed in American women. This tendency in our men and in our women has probably the same origin. In a new country and in a society whose fundamental principle is equality, the individual man is inadequate to any great task. Individual weakness finds its sole remedy in combination. This is quite as true of women as of men. The earliest combinations of women in our country were formed in the name of religion. If men held meetings and organized associations *to build* new churches, women, on a smaller scale and by quieter methods did precisely the same thing to *furnish* the churches, when built, or to raise funds for educating young men to become pastors of such churches; following these combinations of women in the name of religion came others organized in the name of charity; most of the charities were connected with the churches, and to religion and charity the organized work of women was limited until some noble, self-sacrificing women formed an organization in the name of *freedom*, a name naturally dear to American women. It must be confessed that it was not their own freedom or the freedom or their sex for which these women combined, but they organized a society whose object was to deliver the African race in the United States from slavery. Not until 1848 did women in the United States begin to combine for the amelioration of their own condition. . . .

Since 1848 the work of organization among women has gone steadily forward. It received a great impetus during the war of the Rebellion, from 1861 to 1865, and from the latter date the tendency among American women to organize for the accomplishment of purposes too large to be attained by individual effort has grown to be a characteristic feature of American society. These organizations, in the large majority of instances, are in their beginning purely local, limited to a city or perhaps to a district of a city, to a village or perhaps to a country neighborhood. The local organizations of the same kind, i.e., for the same object, spread and multiply, and the aggregate themselves into county organizations; as similar organizations grow up in different counties the county societies aggregate themselves into state associations and finally state associations existing for the same purpose aggregate themselves into a national body. It is true that in some instances . . . an organization has been affected by persons of one mind and a common motive, living in different parts of our great country, and has at once assumed the dignity of a national

association. This is, however, the rare exception; as a rule national organizations of women result from the union of state associations of a similar character, as the state organizations have first resulted from the union of similar county or local associations. In such local organizations of diverse names and purposes many millions of American women are now enrolled. In their hands are the missionary and charitable enterprises of the churches and the great philanthropies which are independent of the churches. By them the artistic taste and the literary culture of rural communities are nurtured, and by them the social life of cities is rescued from mere vulgar luxury, and is made to serve as an ally of the higher culture.

By them, great reforms which are destined to effect, and which do effect an amelioration of the human lot, regardless of sex, are carried forward. Conspicuous among these are some which have already arrived at international importance—such as the great temperance reform movement, with Frances E. Willard at its head—Society of the Red Cross, whose president, Clara Barton, is hardly less dear to foreign than to American hearts—and the Universal Peace Society, whose hope it is to bring all nations to settle their differences by peaceful arbitration instead of war, and with whose work the names of Lucretia Mott and Julia Ward Howe are intimately associated.

The good that is already accomplished by the organized effort of women in the United States is incalculable, and yet its beneficent results are checked and diminished by the fact that members of one organization are ignorant concerning the work of another organization; that organizations misconceive one another's objects and misunderstand one another's methods.

It has not infrequently happened that ignorance of each other's aims and methods has led to indifference, even to hostility between organizations that were really, though unconsciously, allies.

Thus, there was a time in the history of the temperance reform when its advocates deprecated any association with the advocates of woman's political enfranchisement, thinking the latter movement prejudicial to their own success.

Thus, the advocates of certain moral reforms and the leaders of certain charities have held aloof from the advocates of the collegiate education of women, under the erroneous impression that the higher education would harden the hearts of women and put a barrier between them and other women. Just as the advocates of temperance have learned that the advocates of woman's right, under a republic, to the ballot, were obtaining for them the only instrument by which they themselves could gain their specific ends, so the leaders of charities find that one of the first uses which women make of higher education when they have attained it is to lend it to philanthropy that she may more intelligently apply herself to relieving the condition of the poor and suffering; witness the report of the Association of Collegiate Alumnae on the sanitary construction and care of houses, and also the home established by them in one of the most destitute neighborhoods of New York City, and the number of them who have become trained nurses or physicians.

What I have said will make more intelligible what I desire to say about the National council, which I have the honor to represent. It is intended that its triennial meetings (all of which will, by the terms of its constitution, be held in Washington) shall accomplish several important results.

First: They will make an opportunity for women whose work is along different lines, to become personally acquainted with one another; and also to become acquainted with the purposes and the management of organizations, in which they have no part and from which they have hitherto held aloof.

Second: It is anticipated that out of acquaintance will spring reciprocal sympathy. Women will learn that the different lines along which they work are, however different, after all convergent, and destined to meet in that improved state of human society which all desire. It is neither expected nor desired that, as a result of this discovery, women will leave the work in which they are now engaged and attach themselves to other organizations. Temperament, taste, talents, opportunity, surroundings and circumstances will continue to control women in their selection of the line of work which they will undertake for the common good.

Third: We see that this National council will prove, or rather, that it will illustrate, the correlation of the spiritual forces of society. Is one, for instance, intent on feeding the hungry, nursing the sick and comforting the sorrowing? Industrial education and the opening of new industries to women will largely diminish the number of the hungry and thus leave more food for the inevitable pensioners of society.

Let all opportunities for higher education be opened to women and their enlarged intelligence applied to domestic life will so improve the architecture and the sanitation of homes that the number of the sick will be decreased, and the invalids who remain can have the care of skilled nurses and trained physicians of their own sex. Let women have access to the learned professions as well as to all forms of industry and to all means of education—and though sorrow will not cease, it too, will diminish; for the most greivous sorrows result from sin, and the most common and degrading sins result from ignorance, poverty and helplessness.

Fourth: This illustration of the correlation of the spiritual forces of society cannot fail to exert a great and ultimately commanding influence upon public opinion in our country. The triennial meetings of the National council will be the feminine complement of the congress of the United States. Such meetings will focus public attention, reports of them which the press will convey to all parts of the country will instruct the public mind and they cannot fail to accelerate the progress of every movement which they represent.

Fifth: In these meetings will convene not the mere representatives of states of geographical territory, but in them will meet the representatives of great humanitarian enterprises, of spiritual aspirations, of political and social reforms, or moral and religious movements. As these meetings will not bring together the mere representatives of states and sections, but of causes and movements which have the same significance and the same beneficent effect in all states and in all sections, they cannot but result in cultivating in women and, therefore, in the whole people, that spirit of patriotism and of nationality, by which alone the unity of our great republic can be secured.

Learn More about Sewall

May Wright Sewall's life and times have been examined by other authors. Hester Anne Hale produced an unpublished biography of Sewall titled "May Wright Sewall: Avowed Feminist," which is available in the Indiana Historical Society's William Henry Smith Memorial Library in Indianapolis. In 1977 Barbara Jane Stephens wrote her doctoral dissertation at Ball State University on Sewall, which was titled "May Wright Sewall (1844–1920)." Sewall detailed her unusual experiences with spiritualism in the book *Neither Dead nor Sleeping* (Indianapolis: Bobbs-Merrill Company, 1920).

After her death in 1920, Sewall left behind letters and other documents about her active life to a variety of institutions in Indianapolis. The Indianapolis–Marion County Public Library has in its collection approximately five hundred letters written to Sewall from 1879 to 1919, along with guest books signed by those who stayed at the home of May and Theodore Sewall. The library has placed the collection on its Web site at http://www.imcpl.org/resources/digitallibrary/maywrightsewall.html.

The manuscript section of the Indiana Division at the Indiana State Library in Indianapolis has in its collection scrapbooks put together by Sewall on the history and activities of the Girls' Classical School. Also, the ISL has telegrams, letters, and other documents relating to Sewall's participation in Henry Ford's peace trip in World War I. Other collections at the state library that shed light on Sewall's life include the papers of Grace Julian Clarke, Sewall's friend and fellow woman's rights pioneer, and the reminiscences of life in Indianapolis by Mary McLaughlin.

The IHS's William Henry Smith Memorial Library has a number of collections from the organizations Sewall was involved in during her life. These include the papers of the Indianapolis Woman's Club and the Indianapolis Propylaeum. The Lilly Library at Indiana University in Bloomington holds the records of the Bobbs-Merrill Company, the Indianapolis publishing firm that released Sewall's book on spiritualism. The collection includes correspondence between Sewall and her editor, Hewitt H. Howland.

A number of books, articles, and Web sites also detail Sewall's life, the history of the woman's rights movement in the United States, and the struggle for world peace. These include the following:

Books

Jerry Apps, *One-Room Country Schools: History and Recollections from Wisconsin* (Amherst, WI: Amherst Press, 1996).

Richard Gause Boone, *A History of Education in Indiana* (1892; reprint, Indianapolis: Indiana Historical Bureau, 1941).

Claude G. Bowers, *My Life: The Memoirs of Claude Bowers* (New York: Simon and Schuster, 1962).

Ruth Brandon, *The Spiritualists: The Passion for the Occult in the Nineteenth and Twentieth Centuries* (New York: Alfred Knopf, 1983).

Ann Braude, *Radical Spirits: Spiritualism and Women's Rights in Nineteenth-Century America* (Boston: Beacon Press, 1989).

Charlotte Cathcart, *Indianapolis from Our Old Corner* (Indianapolis: Indiana Historical Society, 1965).

Eleanor Clift, *Founding Sisters and the Nineteenth Amendment* (Hoboken, NJ: John Wiley and Sons, 2003).

Jennie Cunningham Croly, *The History of the Woman's Club Movement in America* (New York: Henry G. Allen and Company, 1898).

Merle Curti, *Peace or War: The American Struggle, 1636–1936* (Boston: J. S. Canner and Company, 1959).

Elle Carol DuBois, *The Elizabeth Cady Stanton–Susan B. Anthony Reader: Correspondence, Writings, Speeches,* rev. ed. (Boston: Northeastern University Press, 1992).

Sara M. Evans, *Born for Liberty: A History of Women in America* (New York: The Free Press, 1989).

Eleanor Flexner and Ellen Fitzpatrick, *Century of Struggle: The Woman's Rights Movement in the United States* (1959; reprint, Cambridge, MA: The Belknap Press of Harvard University Press, 1996).

Henry Ford, *My Life and Work* (1922; reprint, Salem, NH: Ayer Company, 1993).

William Dudley Foulke. *A Hoosier Autobiography* (New York: Oxford University Press, 1922).

Barbara Goldsmith, *Other Powers: The Age of Suffrage, Spiritualism, and the Scandalous Victoria Woodhull* (New York: Alfred Knopf, 1998).

Ida Husted Harper. *Life and Work of Susan B. Anthony,* vol. 2. (1898; reprint, New York: Arno and the New York Times, 1969).

Judith E. Harper, *Susan B. Anthony: A Biographical Companion* (Santa Barbara, CA: ABC-CLIO, 1998).

Burnet Hershey, *The Odyssey of Henry Ford and the Great Peace Ship* (New York: Taplinger Publishing Company, 1967).

Aileen S. Kraditor, *The Ideas of the Woman Suffrage Movement, 1890–1920* (1965; reprint, New York: W. W. Norton and Company, 1981).

Barbara S. Kraft, *The Peace Ship: Henry Ford's Pacifist Adventure in the First World War* (New York: Macmillan Publishing Company, 1978).

Robert C. Kriebel, *Where the Saints Have Trod: The Life of Helen Gougar* (West Lafayette, IN: Purdue University Press, 1985).

James H. Madison, *The Indiana Way: A State History* (Indianapolis: Indiana Historical Society; Bloomington: Indiana University Press, 1986).

Clifton J. Phillips, *Indiana in Transition: The Emergence of an Industrial Commonwealth, 1880–1920* (Indianapolis: Indiana Historical Bureau and Indiana Historical Society, 1968).

Leila J. Rupp, *Worlds of Women: The Making of an International Women's*

Movement (Princeton, NJ: Princeton University Press, 1997).

Otis Skinner, *Footlights and Spotlights: Recollections of My Life on the Stage* (Indianapolis: Bobbs-Merrill Company, 1924).

Anna Garlin Spencer, *The Council Idea: A Chronicle of Its Prophets and a Tribute to May Wright Sewall, Architect of Its Form and Builder of Its Method of Work* (New Brunswick, NJ: Heidingsfeld Company, 1930).

Elizabeth Cady Stanton, Susan B. Anthony, and Matilda Joslyn Gage, eds. *History of Woman Suffrage,* vol. 3 (1886; reprint, Salem, NH: Ayer Company, 1985).

Justin E. Walsh, *The Centennial History of the Indiana General Assembly, 1816–1978* (Indianapolis: Select Committee on the Centennial History of the Indiana General Assembly, 1987).

Geoffrey C. Ward and Ken Burns, *Not for Ourselves Alone: The Story of Elizabeth Cady Stanton and Susan B. Anthony* (New York: Alfred Knopf, 1999).

Harriet G. Warkel, *The Herron Chronicle* (Bloomington: Indiana University Press, 2003).

Doris Weatherford, *A History of the American Suffragist Movement* (Santa Barbara, CA: ABC-CLIO, 1998).

Marjorie Spruill Wheeler, *One Woman, One Vote: Rediscovering the Woman Suffrage Movement* (Troutdale, OR: NewSage Press, 1995).

Nancy Woloch, *Women and the American Experience* (1984; reprint, New York: McGraw-Hill, 1994).

Articles

Dwight Clark, "A Forgotten Evanston Institution: The Northwestern Female College," *Journal of the Illinois State Historical Society* 35 (June 1942).

Leigh Darbee, "Focus: '—and ladies of the club': The Indianapolis Woman's Club at 125," *Traces of Indiana and Midwestern History* 12 (Spring 2000).

Eva Draegert, "Cultural History of Indianapolis: Literature, 1875–1890," *Indiana Magazine of History* 52 (September 1956).

Wilbur D. Peat, "History of the John Herron Art Institute," *Bulletin: John Herron Art Institute* 63 (October 1956).

Pat Creech Scholten, "A Public 'Jollification': The 1859 Women's Rights Petition before the Indiana Legislature," *Indiana Magazine of History* 72 (December 1976).

Louis Martin Sears, "Robert Dale Owen as a Mystic," *Indiana Magazine of History* 24 (March 1928).

Anna Stockinger, "The History of Spiritualism in Indiana," *Indiana Magazine of History* 20 (September 1924).

Susan Vogelgesang, "Zerelda Wallace: Indiana's Conservative Radical," *Traces of Indiana and Midwestern History* 4 (Summer 1992).

Web sites

History Channel, The History of Women's Suffrage in America, http://www.history.com/exhibits/woman/main.html.

Library of Congress, Votes for Women, Selections from the National American Woman Suffrage Association Collection, http://memory.loc.gov/ammem/naw/nawshome.html.

National Women's Hall of Fame, http://www.greatwomen.org/.

National Women's History Project, http://www.nwhp.org/.

Public Broadcasting Service, *Not for Ourselves Alone: The Story of Elizabeth Cady Stanton and Susan B. Anthony,* http://www.pbs.org/stantonanthony/.

The Susan B. Anthony Center for Women's Leadership, http://www.rochester.edu/SBA/index.html.

Woman's Rights National Historical Park, Seneca Falls, New York, http://www.nps.gov/wori/.

Index

LAWRENCEBURG PUBLIC LIBRARY
150 MARY STREET
LAWRENCEBURG, IN 47025